FORTRESS
SOREK

D. MICHAEL CARRIERE

*Conflict is inevitable
in every kingdom....
including your own.*

FORTRESS
SOREK

TATE PUBLISHING
AND ENTERPRISES, LLC

Published by Tate Publishing & Enterprises, LLC
127 E. Trade Center Terrace | Mustang, Oklahoma 73064 USA
1.888.361.9473 | www.tatepublishing.com

Tate Publishing is committed to excellence in the publishing industry. The company reflects the philosophy established by the founders, based on Psalm 68:11,
"The Lord gave the word and great was the company of those who published it."

Book design copyright © 2013 by Tate Publishing, LLC. All rights reserved.
Cover design by Jan Sunday Quilaquil
Interior design by Mary Jean Archival

Published in the United States of America

ISBN: 978-1-62295-422-3
1. Fiction / Fantasy / Historical
2. Fiction / War & Military
13.05.07

DEDICATION

To the United States Marine Corps,
especially Gunnery Sergeant Jesus
Lieutenant Jim and his team,
and to all members of the United States
Armed Forces and our allies
who serve and have served for the sake of others.

ACKNOWLEDGMENTS

All of us incur debts of gratitude. Mine begins with my family. My wife, Annette, our children—Allison; Aaron and his wife, Emily; Justin and his wife, Kelsey—and my sister, Lisa. All of them contributed positively to this endeavor.

To three outstanding doctors, Melissa, Christine, and Reem, who collectively worked diligently to save my life, which, among other things, allowed me to finish this book and keep on living.

To Brad whose skill refined the work.

Tina Bayne for designing the map.

Erin

May you use your
giftedness to be a
blessing to many
people as you live
your life.

May God guide you
in all your ways

Mike

CONTENTS

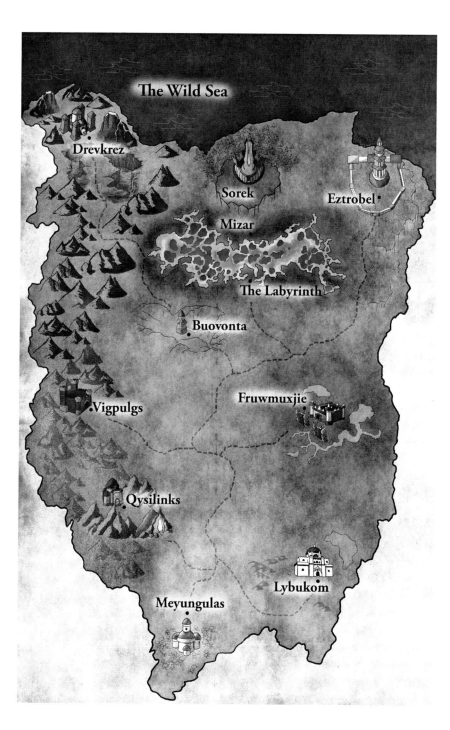

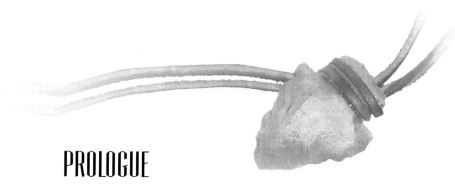

PROLOGUE

The following is a partial recounting of nine kingless kingdoms, carried along by currents of histories past, replicating cycles of conflict, deceit, and mistrust.

However, a few within the vortex are drawn instead into eddies of love, which offer better promises than those anchored in the brutish past.

They seek release from long-established prisons of tradition, precedent, and treachery, the seeds of which have blown throughout their histories and germinate to this very day.

MEDIOCRE EVENING

A brisk breeze bends the light-green grass in rhythmic waves. It also aids the flutterers along their erratic flight, so Ilistra's diminutive hands can't capture even one of them.

"Shall we help her try to catch one, Jovar?"

"No. It's part of what being a child means. Enjoying the challenge."

Instant mazes are being formed as Ilistra wings her way through her own flight of imagination and excitement.

After sitting down to a light lunch, the three companions wander down the creek and inspect the *occinal* orchard in its march toward harvest, then off toward the valley and the compact house called home.

"I can't be late. It's two days' ride from here, and I need to leave in an hour." After readjusting collective expectations, Jovar gathers his belongings, swings them over his shoulder, and walks toward Dohar, tying them securely to the saddle.

Zalin and Ilistra both meander toward their well-worn positions to peer down the road and wave their good-byes. With firm hugs and light kisses, Jovar retreats, and leather rubs leather. Dohar instantly responds to the light touch of the reins, and they watch their husband and father ride back to his station. Hooves stir up the dust and repeat the familiar cadence heard so often from their perch on the knoll.

⬯

The eastern ritual, although barely visible, begins to unveil the all-too-familiar scene—wisps of smoke, obedient slaves of the slightest breeze, bring their scent of battle to all nostrils, friend and foe alike.

The unfolding grim reality is sharply interrupted by a question.

"How many?"

"Twelve dead, eighteen missing, and three captured, sir."

Anger and resolve rush to the surface of the will for an unnumbered time. Why do these creatures always come at night? Why do they never give up? Why do they never show mercy? Questions void of valid answers. The task of burying, healing, and evaluating respond to the necessity of circumstance.

Turning and retreating to the sanctuary, Madnak determines yet again to end this incessant madness by whatever means necessary.

"Call the officers into the Sanctor."

"Yes, sir. At once, sir."

As Madnak enters the expansive structure, his eyes fasten on the object of his scorn, the Fortress Sorek (the stronghold of the Mizar).

High above the surrounding geography, spilling outward toward its victims, lies the plague of Buovonta. Seemingly impenetrable, without any obvious vulnerabilities, it mockingly stands as a proud monument of total domination. An adversary that must be defeated for the sake of all who want to live without dread as a constant unwanted companion.

It isn't known how or when this scourge came to inhabit the high place, but it had been theirs for as long as history has spoken. All attempts at removing this generational horde over countless endeavors by those that lie within the vales and shadows of the kingdom of the Mizars have failed. Despite size, intensity, or resolve, ventures against the stone-hearted vipers proved both fruitless and catastrophic. Past alliances have fared no better, with too many spats on tactics, procedures, timing, and, of course, leadership. Unlike entities have a tendency, as in the animal world, to distrust each other for real or imagined reasons. One would envision having a common enemy would be enough motivation to cooperate more fully, but thus far not so.

The gathered officers sit silently in a stretched circle facing one another, the mosaic of the various kingdoms tiled with perfection in an oblong sphere, engulfing much of the floor. All glance occasionally at the silent indicator of the responsibilities and challenges required of them.

Speaking begins clockwise from the Sanctor's north arch and only when instructed to do so.

"Prince Madnak, all performed fearlessly, charging the enemy and securing the perimeter, protecting the north gate. Captured one enemy and one sword. One *sodus* died from decapitation."

The mention of the captured sword caused a wave of mostly invisible yet noticeable excitement washing

over the seated fighters. Eyes lightened in anticipation. Almost all in the elliptical felt the same. The reports came in order, succinct and without sensation.

When the commentary fell to the first *consor*, Jovar, it was not without internal turmoil, yet no outward expressions betrayed that piece of information.

"Prince Madnak, two *sodii* were killed in quadrant 17, section 4, from enemy infiltration."

With the report completed, he rises, exiting the cavernous room in measured cadence. As the footsteps echo below, the etched archway above reproves the now-fallen warrior, "Mediocrity and failure lead to extinction." He places the azure insignia on the table to his left and passes under the arch. Before exiting the massive ornate building, his mind has already calculated the hours he has left to make his choice—before dawn on the third day.

D. Michael Car

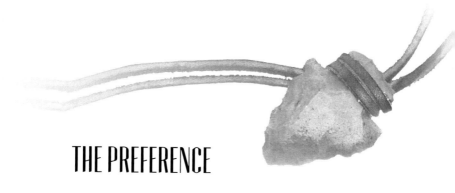

THE PREFERENCE

"Daddy, Daddy."

Jovar embraces Ilistra with somber hugs and a betraying smile of serenity. Zalin plays "all is well" through a hastily prepared meal and engages in conversations of supreme interest to young ears and still-younger hearts. She briefly muses of how uncomplicated life was in her unfolding days when she was that daughter. How the unknown world that existed beyond the walls of her sheltered cove of ignorance was irrelevant. But in the awful present, Jovar had to make a decision in a matter of hours. Countless consors before him had the identical conundrum, including Zalin's own father. To choose either to lead a charge against an overwhelming enemy, or to enter the Dark Emerald Labyrinth are both equally destined to lead to death.

After recounting the story of Galdering, the heroine of Calsweold, Ilistra is quite content with the story's predicable and memorized ending. The tired child closes her eyes in restful calm. Kanka, her favorite, is clenched in a loving embrace. Her benevolent owner begins drifting off into another day of playing in the fields, doing great leaps, inventing a new game, or beginning other fantastic adventures.

The pained dialogue began with the predicable question: "Jovar, what are you going to do?"

He looks at his faithful companion and asks, always expecting an answer, "What do you think I should do?"

Pretence has ended, with Ilistra now sleeping in unconcerned satisfaction.

"I don't know. I just don't know. I don't want you to choose either. It's unfair and cruel. You have served without incident for eight years, but now it's as if you haven't done anything for Konquid."

Jovar was fully expecting that response and had already formulated a reply.

"Zalin, you know very well this is the only way we can possibly survive. We simply can't fail, and if any one of us does, it jeopardizes us all. There really is no other way."

The room turns necessarily pensive.

Zalin's memory abruptly wings back to her day of discovery—the moment of unadorned truth, the occasion her innocence and belief in a world filled with only laughter and play was forever lost.

One nameless afternoon, her mother, Nesigil, gathers Zalin and younger brother Filoquaid to sit down so they could have a chat. It had been over two weeks since the family had seen Hilophil, their father. He had been gone for similar periods of time before. But her mother looked at them with an unfamiliar face and said in deliberate tones, "We may not see your father again."

The siblings looked at each other in stunned silence and disbelief. What was she talking about? This made no sense at all. How could that possibly be true? In fact, it was prophetic.

They never did see him again.

Mother didn't mention in any helpful detail why this could or would be the new uncertain reality for the family. She only repeated the same statement several times, occasionally replying they would just have to wait and see how things turned out. They were to find out the answers to their myriad of questions when it came time to be married, which was yet over a decade away.

Zalin also came to realize after that encounter revelation in Konquid that it is often delivered in sudden, unpredictable jolts, a journey of the surreal. What may seem improbable or even impossible can transform itself into the next version of reality within several scant moments. Leaving Zwenvestin for Belignost was one such epiphany.

Every child is first brought to the Center for Gradual Knowledge at the age of six. Because of the obvious trauma of leaving family, the process begins as day trips to experience unveilings that were unknown up to that point. The initial visits are to the *biosal* farms where various creatures can be held and petted. These included *squalingas*, bright-yellow, feathered, wingless birds; *prelivins*, loose-skinned rodents; and *magi quills*, rotund creatures with long, bluish-green, soft quills. Their various functions and habitats were explained in easy-to-understand language as well as their value to the larger scheme of things.

The whimsical Wisgraf closely follows, a character who weaves a literary yard of fabric with the ease of

the most proficient artisan, intertwining the factual and fantastic with such seamless grace that one could easily forget which was which. The verbal tapestry that emerges is both memorable and magical, a unique work of art that remains in the heart for a very long time, a seed planted in fertile Buovontan soil that produces an abundant crop every season of the year in Selbon Konquid.

The young boys and girls are quietly scrutinized as the education proceeds throughout their young lives. When they are eight, they begin a segregated life based on gender, first for an initial month away from their parents, then to a measured sequence of three months away, followed by one month back home until all the students are assigned to their place and function within the kingdom.

Because the preservation of the realm is paramount, the most promising boys are segregated yet again by age twelve to hone the leadership skills observed by those overseeing their future obligations.

The gifted girls are also examined and segregated in the same way as the boys, but rather than being trained for combat, they are groomed to assume management roles to fill the voids caused by the large demand for sodii. Generally administrative in nature, they will oversee many of the daily organizational demands of the territory.

☙

Zalin bolts out of her daydream as Jovar breaks the silence with hammered resolve. "I'm going to choose the labyrinth. I think it's my best chance at survival."

Zalin instantly reacts. "You want to follow in the steps of my father, who has never returned? You know that only six have ever come back in the history of the choices. I couldn't bear not seeing you again. I still mourn the loss of Father. How could Ilistra and I ever go on?"

The desperation of Zalin was palpable, yet the choice was unavoidable. Death is resolutely imposed on the indecisive—by drowning. Prince Madnak feels it is the most humane way to end one's life. A stone secured around the feet and thrown unceremoniously into the whirlpool is fast and relatively painless; at least that is Madnak's assumption. Who is there to verify whether it is or not so? It doesn't matter. It is a decree.

Jovar looks deep into his wife's frantic eyes, his piercing dark-brown-eyed gaze trying to reassure his wonderful companion that somehow it will all end blissfully.

"You know that one of the reasons I have been successful all these years is that I am very resourceful and have cheated death many times over. This will be no different. When I return with the fresh *ligith* branch, I will be given my life back with honor and be able to retire as a *prosalutar*. I have this sense of destiny in my heart, and I truly believe I will return one day."

Zalin's own heart feels as if it's going to burst at any moment. The deep chasm of grief is overpowering her desperate need for hope. Her spirit fights intensely to find the resolve to somehow escape the powerful internal whirlpool engulfing her faith. To believe this sudden nightmare will come to a satisfactory conclusion lies well beyond her grasp.

Living daily within the shadow of evil and confronting it with weapons and resolve is an undertaking of body, soul, and spirit. An unrelenting adversary demands a mind-set that under better skies would not be necessary. Unfortunately, to insist on perfection from the imperfect is to assure that some will fail.

Yet the circumstances require unwavering resolve, no matter what the personal cost to anyone or everyone. It is the only path to survival in the present and possible freedom in the future. With limited euthanasia, many more lives are rescued and preserved, which bestows at least the hope that someday the horrendous terror will itself finally die.

With no desire to travel again over the chosen road, Jovar and Zalin attempt to fall into improbable sleep. The wind taps an erratic message against an open shed door, and warm air engulfs the bedroom. Both act as a makeshift clock, reminding them of precious moments slipping away. Occasional embraces and hand clasping only amplify the erosion of time, rather than impede it.

The anticipated knock on the *cons ponder* door jolts the couple upright precisely as the *solbon* arises to this day of clouded fate.

CONFRONTING DESTINY

As Jovar grasps the heavy, dark metal handle, he opens to a hulk of a man, filling the opening.

"Have you made your decision, *qualung*?" the brusque voice within the form asks.

"The labyrinth."

"Very well."

A very large hand motions Jovar to follow him to the waiting procession to escort him to the rim of his fate. There is no time given to embrace anything but the present.

Ilistra will have to endure the same ache and mystery that her mother endured as her father stepped out of her life and into the unknown.

Zalin chooses a different location to watch her husband begin the journey down an unfamiliar path, one which may never lead back to this spot of departure. Their final moment together was a brief brush of their hands and a longer embrace with their eyes.

The code of silence permeating the public arena within Buovonta sharpens other senses to observe and absorb the immediate world. The point to disembark, at least for Jovar, is a six-day marathon east. The mixed rhythm of several dozen hooves beating their unhurried yet steady tempo, flinging the well traveled earth

upward, would be soothing and melodic, if it weren't for the present situation. Yet one venue that remains unshackled is the mind's realm.

"Use both hands to strike the enemy. Keep your sword in line with your forearm."

It is an instruction in the art of killing. Although this faux combat occurs as regularly as the beating of one's heart throughout the kingdom, it is somewhat disjointed when it's your own father overseeing the untested warriors.

"Always keep your enemy in front of you."

Learning to keep one's life while ending another is a serious art form. Survival is not a casual occupation.

"Those who keep calm in the midst of battle live to see another day."

Rawlgoul, a veteran of countless encounters with the Mizar hoards, is one of the best at spilling blood.

"You are to live for your land. They are to die for theirs."

As Jovar later learned firsthand, the mantras spoken in preparation for combat did prove their worth in both expertise and survival. Who better to lead the novices than one who has the scars and experience to prove his words?

It wasn't that Rawlgoul was an uncaring father. He certainly had the proper form with the ones he sired. It seemed as though, however, that substance was somehow absent. Perhaps because showing public affection was strongly discouraged, private expressions were also avoided. Knowing how to kill was his job. What else would be expected?

He did in fact smile, occasionally, and sit in the same room and ask common questions of interest to him from time to time. His wife, Xenvel, was similarly emotionally distant from the children as well. To say they loved their progeny would certainly be open to interpretation by those on the receiving end of the interchanges.

The inevitable mandatory assigning of all in the kingdom to the station and position deemed most valuable for the common good affects the emotional climate. On any given day, a sibling can be escorted to an unknown posting for further training. Official policy is for the husband and wife to move together with the balance of the children until all are assigned. Dismantling the family piecemeal does, in fact, create emotional fractures of the whole.

The system isn't conducive for forming strong interpersonal bonds. But desperate measures require desperate action. Jovar couldn't precisely remember the last time he had seen any one of his family, had no idea where they were or even if they were all still alive. As it happened, he was first to be assigned, so how could he know the disposition of his immediate bloodline?

Yet the incredible bonds wrapping Zalin and Ilistra around his heart were more powerful than any weapon forged in the furnaces of Yel Corum. To be bound in a realm that exhibits only stern loyalty denies that breathed air has anything to do with existence. The hardened shell of impassioned performance and fidelity to external welfare was generations in the making. No doubt it would be generations in dismantling, if such impossibilities could somehow exist. It was inconceivable to them that they were unique in this deep embrace of love. Yet to share such passion openly was viewed as a serious breach in the wall of resolve.

Why was perpetual emotional austerity the sole epitome of unmatched strength? Only a fool would try to put love to death. But in the practical sense, only love of duty was paramount in policy and polity. *Superfluous love* appears as an unofficial, misplaced verb in the collective vocabulary of the citizenry, resembling a museum artifact of some distant, ancient culture. Couldn't the unyielding advocates use more than a little acquaintance with love? What would life be like if all were mirrored images of Jovar and his family? Would their collective love weaken the kingdom and make it more vulnerable to decay? For that matter, could their spirit by some implausible turn of events have an impact on the fiends from Sorek?

⌇

Day four of the military caravan brings heavy winds and rains, impeding progress and comfort.

"We'll stop here," orders the gravelly voiced commander.

The modest-built *xilons* every few miles were mainly for such circumstances, to provide shelter and rest for horses and humans alike. The facilities are open to all citizens, but if a shortage of space occurs, priority is given to the government.

This time no one has to be inconvenienced. There is ample room for all, and two hovels remained uninhabited. When proceeding under an emergency situation, delivering a prisoner on his due date is preferred but not mandatory if reasonable conditions prevent the date to be fulfilled.

The temporary habitats are sparse, with no locks on the doors nor food inside. They are not granaries, but only wooden caves designed to keep one out of the weather. All have fireplaces and prove valuable on this day, to dry out drenched clothing and warm chilled skin. The facilities are kept in good repair by mobile teams who have the skills necessary to renovate what needs mending.

Usually comprised of five wagons, they traverse a circuit that on average takes one year to complete. There are twenty-five official routes, so a team can spend over half their life without ever seeing the same place twice. The repairers are easily identifiable by both clothing and equipment, often referred to as the traveling *sanifligs* for their flair for working quickly and with zeal.

Because it appeared that the deluge would last at least for several hours, if not the entire day, food was made available ahead of schedule so there would be no unnecessary stops later. Water, dried meat, and dried fruit were the permanent menus between assignments for ease of distribution. Several days' worth of additional supplies was always carried for various unexpected emergencies.

Jovar finds a secluded spot to eat in an unoccupied xilon and quickly meanders back in his mind to his unexpected emergency and the probable cause. Despite the massive walls surrounding all of Buovonta, occasionally the opponents penetrate the defenses unseen.

Obviously, no one knows how that is accomplished. When inside Buovonta, they evidently hide in the wilderness and wait to join a coordinated attack at a strategic gate or tower. How that is synchronized also remains a mystery. To add to the consternation, they wear uniforms of Buovonta, removed from their prey from previous battles.

It's clear Mizar hoards are present when the death toll in a battle on a wall suddenly rises. Each consor attempts to keep diligent track of his sodii at all times. When several *inbengs* come up unexpectedly missing, he immediately calls for a retreat to see his men face-to-face. The reserves rush up to fill the gaps as the combatants come down off the wall. A secure perimeter around the battle area is formed as soon as the fighting commences, which includes civilians who are in the combat zone. No one is permitted to breach the line until after the battle has ended, which comes just before daylight. All the sodii must remain inside the perimeter until the consors inspect each of their troops.

All fallen sodii are positively identified by the consor before being taken away, so the infiltrators apparently rid themselves of the uniforms and blend back in with the civilians within the security arc. The chaos of battle and the limited night vision would lend itself to that scenario. There is, however, a persistent belief that some of the Mizars, because they look in outward appearance as other Buovontans, have integrated themselves into every aspect of society, patiently waiting to strike when the opportunity presents itself. Then simply go about their lives after the battles, patiently waiting for the next opening to do more damage.

In an unusual breach of tradition, his thoughts are severed by the sudden appearance of the owner of the voice in the doorway.

"Why do you seem so calm? All of the others we have ushered were far more nervous. Are you unaware of where you are going?"

Jovar, somewhat startled by the sudden engagement, turns to face the voice. After a few moments of reflection, Jovar responds to the *fangore* with a tranquil tone and demeanor, "Yes, sir, I do know where I am going. But I believe I will return. I can't explain why, but I have an inner peace that I will survive."

Not fully convinced his prisoner is fully lucid, the questioner continues, "I assume you are aware that only six others have returned to Buovonta, and all had to be moved to the Lashsborg facility for everyone's safety."

Jovar shifts his body slightly away from the questioner, looking eastward toward his still-unseen destination and replies softly, "Yes, sir, I am aware of that also."

The fangore abruptly turns, terminating the brief discussion, and marches briskly toward the rest of the contingent.

Most voyagers were on mundane passages. Only a minority of people passing through were in Jovar's predicament—a very small minority. But the clothing of the escorts plainly identified the mission in progress as well as the transgressor, who wore his official uniform minus the azure insignia of leadership. No

words were necessary to explain to the sighted what was transpiring. Jovar also quickly rises and returns to his place in the procession.

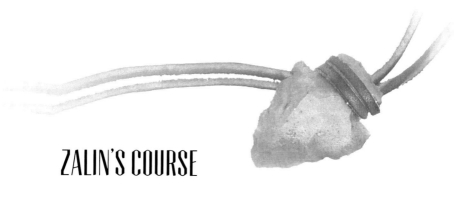

ZALIN'S COURSE

Weeping deep within her pillow, Zalin's grief appears to have no respite. The reservoir of anguish, spilling beyond the fullness of her heart unto her headrest, is not capable of emptying its bottomless contents. Suddenly living her personal nightmare is incredibly numbing, far more crushing than she had ever envisioned. How did her mother keep her composure so well? She knew at that moment she was not, at least in this instance, as strong as her mother. Her mother surely loved her father as deeply as she loved Jovar. How did she find the inner strength to go on?

Wisgraf's impartial voice enters the chaos, "*There is no substitute for experience.*" How could she face her innocent daughter with this tragic news? How could she even begin to utter the unspeakable sorrow for both of them? Thankfully, Ilistra usually sleeps well into the morning, granting more time to plan something credible.

Getting some fresh air full in her face may help dry up the torrent. Meandering outside parallel to Ilistra's window so she can hear her daughter seemed logical at the moment. Grasping a thin scarf on the way out the door to use as a muffle should keep the deluge from awakening sleeping ears.

The cool and brisk dark breeze helps slow the grieving cascade. Trying to form a list of options while listening for her soon-to-be-knowledgeable daughter was a contrast of wills. Her mother may have taken the path of hopeless hope, dangling the minute possibility of a future reunion from the thread of frayed reality. What would hurt the least? Being brutally and totally frank, stabbing the heart with one great thrust of an enormous sword? Or shading the route of reason with a camouflage of half-truths?

Her own wounded heart knew the answer all along. To hear of a continued enjoyable future was far better than the ship crashing full force on the rocks, where only wreckage remains. *Hope in the heart is a treasure worth saving.* For Ilistra's sake, the partially veiled road would be traveled on, at least for the present.

Ilistra bounds into the tiny kitchen in late morning, ready to eat her breakfast—fresh eggs, fresh milk, and fresh sausage compliments of the recently dispatched *fogol*.

"Mommy, what are we going to do today? I would really like to go to the pond and watch the *squivnons* swim and fly away when we get too close."

"Okay, dear, that sounds like a fun thing to do."

Zalin had long since learned how to be something she wasn't. Only Jovar knew what was truly in her heart and spirit. Her other acquaintances assumed she was just as detached from others outside her own families as they were. Knowing a name is not the equivalent as knowing the named.

Formal emotional distance is accepted policy, except for the military, who have necessary survival relationships. Keep focused on the need to serve the greater good makes controlling outcomes much easier. Neat and uncomplicated. How often Zalin heard the official policy. However, she and Jovar viewed this outlook as having a bond without the adhesive. The standard argument of "the kingdom is still in existence" was not, nor would ever be, their official policy.

"Mommy, where is Daddy?" the young voice asks when she doesn't see her father appear at the pond. He is often out in the barn before Ilistra and her mother eat breakfast, but when he doesn't come in a timely matter, something must have happened.

"Well, dear, your father was called back to Zwenvestin Linrox in the middle of the night for an emergency and will be gone for a while."

Unaccustomed to lying to anyone, especially her own daughter, Zalin simultaneously feels her face flush and an unusual flutter in her stomach. Thankfully, Ilistra was looking away when asking that question. Sudden departures had occurred before and after Ilistra's birth, so there would be no cause for alarm, just the usual missing of her father until he returned on Dohar. Having a few weeks now to plot her next course of action, Zalin's initial plan is to wait for several weeks when Ilistra asks about her father again. She would then plant another nonfact in her daughter's mind.

Lies have the advantage of being either spontaneous or calculated. Having an infinite variety of choices and not being constrained by all the facts, deception can dock anywhere it pleases. Truth, however, has specific explanations and destinations and anchors only in predetermined harbors. In the meantime, life was to go on as if everything was just fine, when in fact, nothing was.

MADNAK

Prince Madnak has initially addressed the conse-quences of the recent attack, having promoted *valins* to replace the five consors. He then turns his attention to the three captured alive. Proceeding by horseback to the secluded Acnonicad, he observes several of the workmen replacing a portion of the stone-slab roofing of a military building and repairing a large, wooden beam support, which has sustained fire damage.

Among the plentiful assault arsenal employed by the Mizars is a device that hurls sturdy fiery cylinders, which burst on impact. They are filled with a thick, tarlike substance whose origin is from distant portions of the swamps within the labyrinth. These flaming missiles resemble a streaking comet and cause considerable damage and horrid death to anyone unfortunate enough to be hit by them. Dispensed far out of archery range, the sites have to be attacked quickly. But before any sodii can come anywhere near these weapons, they cease firing, thereby not betraying their exact positions. When investigating suspected sites the following day, no sign of the fearsome weapons are found.

The night gives additional advantage to the horde. Attacks only come with a fully overcast sky, with no moon to light either's path. The pack of vermin clothes themselves in black from head to foot and smear dark mud over all exposed skin. They literally lie in wait in dispersed intermittent squads, saturating the battlefield, waiting until the sodii come within range or pass by. Attack comes silently and without warning. No speaking or yelling. The effect unsettles even the most weathered veteran of nocturnal combat. Sodii advance steps from one another, and without notice, one of them will hear a slight sound, only to turn around to see his comrade lying dead on the ground. Usually a slit throat or a long, bladed knife slipped expertly into the heart. The battle wages in this bizarre silent fashion until a bone-chilling shout from all over the battlefield suddenly erupts, instantly unleashing the furor of the gleaming swords against those in the field and unto the fortress itself.

No weapon ever seen by any of the kingdoms compares to these. So sharp that even touching them on their edges with a finger will cause blood to flow. The metal so flawless that none can imagine how they are made. Practically unbreakable yet extremely light and perfectly balanced, even a younger novice proves a challenge for a seasoned swordsman. The fields of daylight after every battle speak silent testimony to their deadly effectiveness.

When one is recovered, it is reason to celebrate, although it is never expressed in that fashion. All consors know that one of them will have the privilege of wielding the enemy's weapon against their enemy. The preferred goal is to kill in kind, death by decapitation, the Mizars' favorite means of execution. No mercy is shown, unless ordered by the prince, because the Mizars show none. However, if any consor loses that weapon in battle to the enemy and lives, the penalty is public execution that same day at noon: "With high honor comes higher responsibility."

ᏩᎢᎢᎲᏪᏅ

Continuing along the paved granite roadway, the various trees and flowers, long since awakened from the sleep of winter, display their beauty in unabashed glory. By early afternoon, Price Madnak arrives at the walled compound and enters through the high ornate arch, which announces in silent, blue-green stone, Acnonicad. Passing by myriads of ancient structures, previous homes of the privileged few now serve as very comfortable dwellings of the captured enemy.

Proceeding to the *forgal's* office, the prince enters unannounced. The forgal, examining various documents on his expansive marble-topped desk, immediately rises to greet the prince.

"Very good to see you again, Prince Madnak. How may I be of service to you?"

Learning from past encounters, the forgal doesn't assume the nature of the visit, although it always concerns the prisoners.

"I would like to know what you have learned from the most recent captures." It is precisely the wording the prince always responds to the invitation to help.

"Of course, sir. Would you like to visit in the office or out in the yard?"

"We will talk along the way to the housing areas."

There is another verbatim rejoinder. "Very well. Shall we proceed?"

The forgal, besides being the overseer of the compound, is also fluent in Fajixa. He is one of the translators that work with the prisoners on an ongoing basis.

The cold stone walkways meander as multifaceted streams, a gleaming accent to the flowers, plants, shrubs, and low-growing trees that line the paths. The residences are quite beautiful, with exquisite designs gracing doorways and window frames, all constructed of exotic stone imported from other friendly kingdoms.

They approach a larger residence on a secluded walkway and knock firmly on the wooden carved door. A large *lolinin* tree provides ample shade to the home. After a brief interlude, a young man answers the door.

"Hello, Rafon. This is Prince Madnak, the overseer of Buovonta."

Rafon extends his hand in greeting and invites the duo inside.

"Prince Madnak is here to ask you several questions. You will remember that I spoke of this with you two weeks ago and mentioned we would be joining you."

As the trio retires to several comfortable, leather-cushioned chairs, Prince Madnak begins with a simple inquiry.

"How long have you been a Mizar warrior?"

"This was actually my first mission. I have been training for seven years and was anxious to join the battle for freedom."

"What battle for freedom are you referring to, Rafon?"

"Well, the battle to free all the citizens of Buovonta, of course."

"What makes you think that the citizens of Buovonta need freedom?"

"This is the only mission we have," replies Rafon.

This is precisely the message the prince has heard time and again—coming to set the captives free. The answer doesn't ring true. How does killing the ones you are claiming to rescue benefit them? Is this just a morbid calculation of collateral damage? Some survive, but most are killed? The prince has managed to control his responses over the years because experience has discovered it is far more effective to gather information through comfort rather than coercion. Ironic as it may be, the prisoners have better food, water, and shelter than the vast majority of Buovontans.

This, of course, wasn't always the preferred practice. The usual forms of torture were applied for several centuries, beginning with threats and minor pain to gradually increased methods and techniques of affliction until they either confessed or died in one of many gruesome ways. This would yield some results, but many later proved to be false or misleading. Therefore, tactics were gradually designed in the opposite direction until it became the reverse of previous strategies. Although nothing has changed on the battlefield, nor in military tactics, it did begin to yield interesting information from time to time.

None outside the interrogation team knows what goes on in Acnonicad. Besides, the day will come when all the prisoners will become negotiating items and useful object lessons if the enemy doesn't respond in good faith. For the present, all is calm and friendly, at least externally. Buovonta has never really trusted the enemy and probably never will. The prevailing opinion is that this mind-set is mutual on both sides. The reports of the six who have returned with the ligith branch have reinforced this belief. If feigning cordiality produces results over time, so be it.

Prince Madnak begins his journey back to Kilrek, contemplating various scenarios on how to decisively defeat the Mizars. The assumption has always been to overcome their strength with greater strength. However, everyone has weaknesses. Discovering and exploiting the dread enemy's self-inflicted blindness may be the only possible way to fulfill the oft-dreamed dream. The gentle interrogations are primarily designed as listening events. People who don't feel threatened tend to be more liberal in their speech, less reserved, less guarded.

As Madnak has heard so many times before, their stated passion is liberty for Buovonta. *Liberty for Buovonta.* The very mention of that phrase inflames Madnak's very being.

Who has more freedom than Buovontans? What can't they do? Where can't they go? What can't they say?

The only prison is the one imposed on them by the Mizars' relentless fury against Buovonta.

At that moment, Madnak has a sudden inspiration. Was it possible to turn their declared motive against them; to use their self-professed passion as a scent to lead them to destruction? Their weakness may rest

in their own perceived greatest strength. Who truly believes they are weak when they know they are strong? Who feels the need to guard that which is already secured? It will take much thought and preparation to devise a perfect trap. The other kingdoms will have to participate as well, to be certain the pestilence is permanently eradicated. Although specifics have yet to be materialized, Madnak has an inner sense that he may have stumbled onto the basic formula for piercing the heart of the Mizars and delivering a fatal blow— their own best intentions.

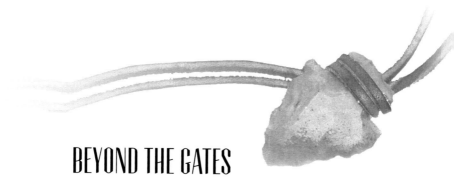

BEYOND THE GATES

It was just approaching evening on the seventh day when the distant walls of the eastern fortifications come into view. Several miles away, the commander decides to keep proceeding until they reach the village and the adjoining outpost. There are barracks there especially designed to their mission. It also brings additional security and good food, commodities that become increasingly valuable the longer one is away from them.

Jovar also sees the wall, both a symbol and reality marking this part of his life drawing to a close. Once the massive doors open for him to exit before the solbon rises, he will truly begin anew. His belief in his personal destiny will commence the moment he and Dohar embark on their journey toward the labyrinth.

The caravan arrives in the still-active village two hours after twilight. The fangore has completed this mission many times before and is greeted by familiar voices.

"Fangore, how many sodii and how many prisoners?"

"There are twelve sodii, myself, and one qualung."

"Very well, please go to barracks five and escort the prisoner to secure unit number two, which is directly across the lane of your barracks. Good to see you again, Fangore Balequo."

"Good to see you as well, Felcon Jelwark."

The horses slowly veer right as they close on Jovar's final resting place before his life forever changes. As the column comes to a halt, the commander orders Jovar to leave his mount to the *motvear* and walk to the doorway of the *goniclis*. As Jovar swings his left leg over Dohar's saddle, Fangore Balequo is doing to same. He always delivers his charges personally, first to the goniclis and then to the gate at next daybreak. Only two taps on the solid plain door, except for the small hole at eye height, are necessary. Within seconds, a uniformed sodus opens the door. The creaking sound of metal hinges welcomes them in.

"This is a qualung prisoner. He will be leaving for the labyrinth at daybreak."

"Yes, Sir Fangore. We will have him ready for you at five o'clock in the morning."

With his mission almost completed, Fangore Balequo turns and shuts the door behind him.

"As you may know, qualung, it is the custom to grant you one letter to write to your family if you choose. However, it must be no more than forty words. Do you wish to write?"

Jovar was unaware of this, but was very happy to have this unexpected opportunity. "Yes, sir, I would."

Apparently it was a solitary drop of grace offered to those who were almost certainly going to die within a few days. At this juncture, he would take favor from whatever source it came from. His mind begins to compose a note, however brief it has to be. He too is coming to the same conclusion as his wife: "Inevitability may require unpleasant choices."

The cell was exactly as one would expect—a well-worn, uncomfortable, straw-filled mat on the stone floor, a bucket for nighttime necessities, and a very small table with a stool. The balance of the room consisted of a lone page of paper on the table lying by an almost empty ink well and a weathered stylus. It would not be difficult to write a chapter, but barely a verse was permitted. After much deliberation and mental editing, a simple message was decided on.

> Ilistra and Zalin,
>
> I am sorry this assignment is going to be longer than expected, perhaps a year or two. I will come back. Be good. Be patient. You will see me return from the east one day.
>
> > Love,
> > Daddy

Jovar tried to ignore the approaching morning and managed to dream himself back into their lives for a short visit. As they were walking through the airy woods to a favorite place to overlook the valley, a voice abruptly shatters the scene.

"Time to leave, qualung."

It was Fangore Balequo, about to complete his most recent task.

Jovar bolts awake with a reflexive, "Yes, sir."

Sleeping in his clothes, as much for warmth as well as for some flimsy barrier against whatever else may be residing with him in this brief residence, he quickly rises to meet the challenge. As the duo walk outside, it still resembles the night, but soon the way to the labyrinth will be fully illuminated.

For the formally condemned, the procedure is to provide a two-week supply of provisions. The trio of water, meat, and fruit had been secured to Dohar earlier that morning. This symbol of executive mercy, a meager and barely negligible supply of sustenance, was jointly a whispered thank-you for faithfulness and a loud rebuke for failure. Even though practically nighttime, despite the technical time of day, an ample supply of sodii were stationed at the gate and on the walls to ensure no sudden attack from the Mizars, despite no evidence of any being present.

Jovar walks with a deliberate gait with Dohar between the double rows of sodii. It resembled a mirrored image of his entry into the ranks of the consors a few years earlier. Although none of his family was in attendance, all of the dignitaries of Fortress Kilrek were present. Standing on either side of the twelve newly minted consors were *fangores* and seasoned consors, welcoming them into the hallowed ranks of their fraternity within Buovonta. Still single and enthusiastic, reaping the fruit of great accomplishments, that was a day to remember.

This one was as well, stepping foot into a completely foreign passageway to begin again. The present somber procession, concluding the final steps of that heady corridor of lofty expectations begun years ago, was ending momentarily at the closed gates of Heoprel.

The funeral, like wordless dirge, comes to a unified halt, barely twelve feet from the double doors. Made from the *jankel* tree, the heaviest hardwood available, the doors are forty-four feet high, and each fourteen feet wide. Six considerable hinges, secured into the three-foot-wide frames around the doors, form an impressive entrance, or in this case, exit. There is also a resin embedded in their grain that is fire resistant. To aid in thwarting the inevitable fiery attacks, they are fully encased in *kakinza* metal, a reddish brown material that is very difficult to penetrate. The impressive edifices, here and at Kilrek, that Jovar defended so vigorously in body and spirit, now ironically demand he leave their protective veneers and venture alone into combat with death's persistent shadowy grasp.

There are no last words, no fond farewells, no syllables of encouragement—just the necessary sounds of their surroundings. Jovar hears the manipulated leaves from a nearby *spinitic* tree being played by the slight breeze. Joining the minute cacophony are the metal-on-metal squeaks of the substantial hinges being forced open to signal the transition.

The doors are designed to open outward to make it more difficult to breach them by applying force against them. As the landscape begins to unfold before him, Jovar can only see the black outline of the horizon, ever expanding with each foot of this new realm being unveiled before him. Within moments, the way is cleared to proceed. Jovar mounts Dohar, the familiar sounds of the creaking leather saddle whispering in the nearly silent scene. With no hesitation and a slight touch on Dohar's flanks, they leave their former home, facing fully the unknown surrounding them.

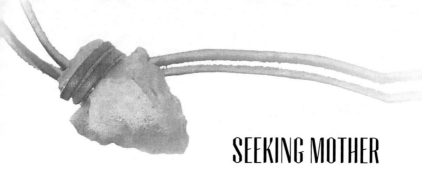

SEEKING MOTHER

As Zalin awakes to the eighth day without her beloved Jovar at her side, the ache in her heart grows more weighty like some malignant intruder into her soul. She will have to find some relief soon, if only for self-survival. The thought of going to her mother's home, who has experienced the same unrelenting agony, may be the place to seek some relief, as temporary as it may be. Although it will take five days of travel, she has no real choice but to respond to her pain. The barn still houses Salib, the plodding yet steady literal worker of the fields. Hitching the small wagon is something Zalin is well versed in, and there is plenty of fresh and dried food to take along. However, attempting to breathe fresh life into one's soul is rather daunting, especially considering one is breathless in spirit.

While preparing Ilistra's favorite desserts, baked *zinying* and *emelicon* bars, Zalin asks the question.

"Honey, would you like to go to Grandmother Nesigil's home to visit for a while? We can hitch up Salib and have a great adventure. We can plan together what we would like to take along. What do you think?"

Ilistra breaks out in a spontaneous giggle, clapping her flour-drenched hands. Grandmother Nesigil's house was one of her favorite places to go.

"Oh, Mommy, that would be wonderful."

A slight sliver of joy pierces the dark mass in her heart, releasing a brief soothing balm to her wounds.

"That's great, Ilistra. I can hardly wait. What about you?"

"Me too, Mommy. We can go and fish in the pond and ride on her pet *fasingbuk* and take walks and play on the hills and everything. When are we going to leave?"

"Probably in a day or two. Just as soon as we can get ready and pack our things and prepare the food for us and Salib."

Zalin suddenly senses something of a surge in energy and purpose despite her longing for Jovar. After all, they do have a lovely daughter in spirit and appearance, and Ilistra needs her mother now more than ever, even though she doesn't realize it yet.

∽∾

Zalin and Ilistra wait patiently at the intersection of their road and the main thoroughfare until a substantial group of travelers pass by. This is practiced in all the kingdoms for safety's sake. They will also stay together in the wooden caves, again as security and refuge from the evening. It is not necessary to know any of the groups personally, given that it is common practice to work together for mutual benefit, whether you know one another or not. It's also traditionally not a festive, interactive event, so conversations tend to be task, rather than interpersonal, in content. The roadways are the main arteries between the kingdoms, so it is relatively safe for all concerned.

On the other hand, the unofficial persistent rumors of secret infiltrations of the dread adversaries run as a shallow tributary through collective subterranean fears. Based in fact or myth? Either scenario plants seeds of doubt. Could someone next to you on the trail or at a meal actually be a Mizar? The subject is never addressed in any personal way because no one who was a Mizar would tell the truth. In addition, they are only nocturnal fighters, so they too could conceivably travel freely during the day, like any other individual or group, carrying their characteristic garb in concealed tow.

Yet the general population imagines the Mizars as wild, untamed, barely above animal status beings, with an uncontrollable spirit. Therefore, unless someone is acting very aggressive and out of their mind, they couldn't possibly be Mizars. Cases of missing people do appear occasionally from time to time, but that happens in any large population base. Follow-up on those instances are left primarily to family members, not the sodii or any other governmental group.

Mother and daughter observe several groups go by, but none were going near Zwenvestin.

Finally, after several more hours, a small band of travelers are heading in their direction. Three young married families, with fourteen children, are also going to see their relatives in that vicinity. As was the custom, there is little discussion about personal matters, only what was deemed necessary for the whole group's satisfaction. Zalin silently assess what she sees and hears and feels they are enjoyable and safe enough to travel with.

From that point on, there is very little discussion, even within the parties that know one another. The group meets several more individuals and small groups going in the direction they had just left. Occasionally, a glance would be offered, and less occasionally, a wave of a hand. How odd it seemed to Zalin that people who looked so amiable could have such a cold-as-stone disposition.

The group approaches a xilon that doesn't appear to be occupied. It's still only midday, and most want to get to their destinations as soon as possible, so very few retire early from their journey. There are also necessity facilities behind the wood caves that are private in nature. All of the travelers take advantage of the xilon and walk and stretch their legs, meandering in small, irregular circles. Because Zalin and Ilistra don't know anyone in the caravan, they slip away and enter one of the empty hovels to rest and eat a light lunch. Zalin, still grieving within her spirit, is yet able to mask her real emotions.

"Ilistra, what do you think we will get to see on this trip?"

Ilistra scrunches her nose and lips, looks upward to nowhere, and suddenly blurts out, "Maybe a *krunun!*"

She had seen one at Belignost and was thoroughly overwhelmed at its very presence. It is such a huge animal who appeared to be ferocious but was one of the most gentle creatures in the kingdoms. Zalin smiled a broad, genuine smile and unexpectedly laughed, not only remembering her first encounter but also appreciating again Ilistra's.

"Joy and sorrow often trade places at a moment's notice," is one of Wisgraf's quotes that are shared with the older children who have lived longer and have drunk deeper from their personal well of experiences. It certainly seemed to fit the occasion. How good it felt to laugh without effort, even for an instant. The spontaneous moment reminds Zalin that she is not alone in the world. There are symbiotic relationships that need constant care.

Within a short time, an internal timepiece alerts everyone to assemble to their places, and the civilian march resumes. Children are the last to learn the art of the rigid official emotional policy. Before long, Ilistra and three other similar-aged girls are slowly communicating in silent gestures. Eyes and faces intermix in a timeless ritual and begin building a bridge to one another, as only children know how to construct. As evening was approaching, the next place of refuge comes into view. It too was sparsely populated.

There were three men to give a sense of security along with several *denfengs* to aid in any defense that might be needed. There were again sufficient empty places to inhabit, so the families naturally went together, leaving Zalin and Ilistra to choose their place of rest.

They had been alone countless times before because of Jovar's responsibilities, but the familiar has its own built-in security. Strange places have an uneasy sense to them whether valid or supposed. They did take solace in having Salib, not as a guard but as a trusted companion, which does help in unsettling times.

Morning comes as scheduled and a collective breakfast casually emerges. Soon there is a bit of nonrequired interchange. Ilistra and her three new acquaintances, Felora, Cesingria, and Juwimil, exchange basic information with one another and begin to chatter as only young girls can. None of the parents seem to mind. Perhaps they feel a bit envious. Caught up in unfettered babble, the innocent, young lives enjoy the moments as if there would never be an end to them. Zalin is just pleased that Ilistra is enjoying the trip and engaging in playful delight.

Being the only husbandless woman with a child is not a signal that there is something amiss. No one would think anything of it, seeing all men are assigned to tasks and may be away from home as often as Jovar was. There would only be discomfort if someone engages her and begins to ask a few questions, as innocent as that usually is.

Unofficial conversation can lead down paths not anticipated or desired. Of course, she isn't planning on telling the truth at any rate. Lying becomes easy, if practiced enough.

"Isn't it wonderful to watch our children play together?"

Zalin turns to see who has engaged her. The questioner has an easy smile and fires a friendly volley, evidently seeing what type of response she might receive from Zalin.

"Why, yes, it is. One of the great pleasures of being a parent," Zalin lobs back in kind.

"My name is Evonquel. May I ask yours?"

"Of course, I'm Zalin."

"Nice to meet you, Zalin."

"I feel the same, Evonquel." Now it's Zalin's turn to initiate the next exchange of information. "Ilistra and I are going to see my mother in Zwenvestin."

"Well, that's quite a coincidence because that is exactly where we are going ourselves."

Zalin experiences a sense of bewilderment as to the forwardness of Evonquel yet feels better just sharing foundational information with someone else, even to a perfect stranger. It seems to have a soothing effect on her spirit.

Zalin continues, "Well, perhaps we can visit each other when we get there. Are you staying long?"

"Well, yes, we are. My husband, Praxis, is assuming a consor's position there."

"That's quite an honor," Zalin hears herself saying to Evonquel. She is suddenly thrust into a mode of automatic response when hearing the word "consor" again. The agony that position brought on them led right to the very ground she is standing on. Still smiling, but this time not genuinely, Zalin replies, "My husband, Jovar, is also a consor, but is gone on a lengthy assignment right now."

It was shocking to hear those words come out of her mouth. The same deception she shared with her own daughter has spread to someone she knows almost nothing about. Wisgraf certainly knew a lot about behavior, good and bad.

"Well, we have a few things in common, don't we?" Evonquel innocently replies.

"Yes, we do."

At that moment, the men speak to their families to gather their belongings and begin preparing for the next leg of the trip. The conversation comes to a sudden stop. Zalin is thankful. She doesn't want to become proficient in deception.

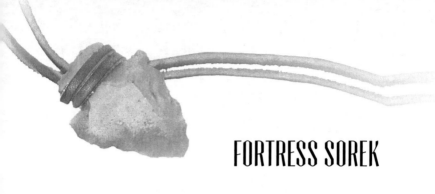

FORTRESS SOREK

Slender plumes of gray-black smoke rise and twirl in the wind. The wispy origins are manifold burning fires, hundreds of feet above the ground. Rows of kilns, arranged in semicircles, border the rim of a massive sandy field. Tempered artisans work methodically to forge weapons of war.

Nexiel, the chief artisan, is fully engaged in the crucial inspection cycle, examining each fresh product of the blazing fires after they have been cooled by large vats of water. Every aspect of its intended function must be flawless, made to exact time-tested standards, using formulas that have been perfected over countless generations. Only if some weakness is uncovered would the practices, techniques, or processes be modified. No significant changes have occurred in over five hundred years.

∞

Vision from the immense plateau is almost beyond description. In every direction on a cloudless day, sight extends to the distant horizon. If standing in the center of the earthen and rock table, the territory below the flattened mound can't be seen until seven miles out. On the north end is a grove of giant *werodod* trees, rising six hundred feet into the air. They form a staggered, oval ring near the base of the fortress and spread east, west, and north several miles until they touch the edge of the Wild Sea. These great sentinels rise upward in glorious fashion and yet at their apex are still slightly below the rim of the Fortress Sorek.

These mighty sentries of chance also serve as a living curtain to one of the great secrets of the fortress. Immediately fronting the massive vegetation on the north face of the mound, commencing at ground level, is a natural fissure that slowly winds and weaves upward until it reaches the top of the fortress. The length of the fissure on the top of the plateau extends two thousand five hundred and thirty-eight yards and averages about five yards wide, which ultimately made possible access to the top.

The forerunners of Sorek realized the value of this priceless find. What greater security could there be? Having an Orwellian's perch high enough to see for over sixty five miles any enemy approaching and a six hundred forty-nine foot-high barrier that is impossible to scale, tear, or wear down, all that was necessary was to build a road to the top.

The project took approximately twenty-nine years to complete. The initial stage began with a stone base and transporting sand from the sea's shore to compact and fill in the crevices of each layer of rock. This base was then overlaid with quarried rock from the north side of their fortress. The frequent rains assure the sand compresses to an almost-rocklike consistency.

Although the road is somewhat steep, narrower wagons were constructed with a sophisticated braking system to go

up and down the road safely. The open fissure on the top is covered completely with uniformly thick *agjolin* beams that are spaced four inches apart to allow natural light on the roadway. A high fence of agjolin provides a barricade around its perimeter to avoid any accidents.

Before the discovery at Sorek, the Mizars were a small itinerant unorganized tribe. But once the citadel had been established, they flourished. Within a century and a half, they grew into an impressive tribe. The high refuge was not, nor is, their primary residence. Although it can easily accommodate all of the residents, the land surrounding the plateau is quite fertile and productive.

Storehouses have long been erected on the High Place, as it is commonly referred to, with a seven-year supply of grain on hand at all times. The oldest grain is consumed each year by the Mizars. Because it keeps so well, there is no appreciable difference between the freshest wheat and its older counterparts. Very large cisterns built over the centuries capture plentiful rainwater each year. The Wild Sea provides a formidable natural defense and creates its own weather patterns, so adequate moisture for land, man, and beasts is assured. Beyond the natural defenses, there is a substantial supply of four-legged carnivores. They both guard the prisoners and are an efficient lethal weapon that strike on command with terrifying speed.

Fertile soil lines the perimeter near the outside rim and the perimeter near the outside rim is actively growing raised vegetable beds; in the event of a lengthy siege, the Mizars could conceivably stay there indefinitely if need be. Spaces between the beds and a two-hundred-foot-wide pathway extending to the very edge of the rim are reserved for military exercises, to repel any and all enemies. A waist-high rock wall follows the outline of the table all around its border to provide a secure boundary. *Nocvals* use gravity to multiply the deadly force of anything hurled down. Many long, barrack-type buildings cover the area reserved for living quarters. Not designed for show, they are very plain yet adequate.

Neither chance nor assumption is an unacceptable attitude. The smallest details of the society are well organized and thorough. Citizens nine years old and above have duties assigned to them by the family *philmons*, but indirectly by the High Council.

These primary overseers are chosen because over the course of their adult lives, they have exhibited exemplary public behavior, have an excellent reputation within the community, and have consistently provided wise counsel to their peers and, at times, to the society at large—chosen by the population of twenty-seven years old and above in public meetings, which are held approximately every six years. This seems to be the natural attrition rate for the council. If several resignations or deaths occur unexpectedly, a meeting is convened in a timely manner. A name will be submitted by a reputable person who will then sponsor the person for consideration. There are no absolute limits concerning the number of individuals on the High Council, but eleven to fifteen has been the historical margins for the past several centuries.

The prince is seen as the overseer of the military facet of the kingdom, but the High Council makes judgments on the balance of items concerning the kingdom's welfare. The leadership of the council itself is done internally. The chosen privos serves at the pleasure of the council and can be changed by their collective authority, but this rarely happens. Wisdom increases, not decreases, with the seasons. The present privos, Vaumond, has been at the post for thirty-two years. There is an unspoken attempt to keep the balance of male and female roughly equal, but the numbers vary from time to time without any dissent. The primary focus is on performance, not gender.

Concerted efforts are made to cultivate, as if young plants, those in the kingdom who display the qualities necessary for the council. Age is always a secondary consideration for leadership, not because of bias but there is no substitute for experience. Those who have lived the longest understand the adage the best. However, when involved in hostilities against various kingdoms who singularly want to destroy you and your way of life, everyone needs to contribute to the common welfare. There will always be a need for outstanding wisdom, regardless of the well from which it is drawn. As Vaumond often quotes, "Those who follow today lead tomorrow."

On ground level, newly minted *syncryses* flash in the bright light of noon, preparing for the actual combat to commence. Those responsible for the details of war stand huddled in close proximity to the maps before them high above their nocvals.

The next assignment is going to be waged against Eztrobel, the kingdom of the Tyvrens. Due east of Sorek, it will be a two-week march. If the weather permits, the attack will start soon after their positions and assignments are established.

"We've always had the best success with diversion. I suggest starting fires here on the west side with our *furens* and simultaneously scaling the east wall with our *eligex* at this point." Coluquo Jezfahr gestures, one of the senior *prevens* to Prince Imixam.

"I believe setting a fire on the south wall here then four volleys of *morvengs* over the western wall there will force them to rush more *kesereks* toward the fire and temporarily evacuate the western wall. This will allow us to use overwhelming force to breach that wall with our *opirsak* at this point." Fegzil Oxrinmun, also a close advisor, steps back into the semicircle and hands the slender pointer back to the keserek.

The discussion continues for another two and a half hours before a consensus is agreed upon by the advisors and approved by Prince Imixam. Although warfare has been a part of the histories of the kingdoms for many generations, there is in the secret places of the assembled hearts a desire that one day it would end. The sacrifices they make personally on the battlefield and the cost to those they love are enormous. No one doubts the value of the purpose of these campaigns, but how much better to have agreement across the kingdoms without the continual killing. However, bloodletting is the sole alternative at present, for without it, there is no peace or security in the kingdom of Sorek.

THE LABYRINTH

As the horizon begins to outline in greater detail the unfolding road, Jovar decides to keep riding east for the present. In half an hour, he will turn north, in the direction of Sorek and the labyrinth. There are many miles of open countryside between the walled fortresses of the nine kingdoms. The land for several miles out from every fortress is cleared of all trees and the ground burned each spring to keep the vegetation at a minimum. Beyond that perimeter lies the various forest lands, and beyond that, the Dark Emerald Labyrinth. The landmass is constructed in such a way that the Fortress Sorek lies in the north central portion of three million acres. Fortress Sorek borders the southern edge of the Wild Sea, effectively becoming its northern border. Unlike the other kingdoms, Sorek has a six-mile security swath, which then butts up to the forest lands.

The labyrinth forms a complete hedge around Sorek, an oblong barrier that contains many hazards and whose overall width averages over sixty miles, although some sections are believed to be well over a hundred miles across. It has depressions, mostly in the central portions of the bogs, which run the entire length of the labyrinth. Dangerous creatures abound.

Most of its vegetation varies from bright to very dark green. The underbrush at the edges of the labyrinth is relatively scattered for the first mile or so, but then vines, low-hanging branches, and almost impenetrable brush mingled with a multitude of trees of all sizes make every few yards a challenge.

The surface water of the bogs hosts very beautiful algae, which has a luminescence quality. It shimmers in the moonlight as if it were a liquid emerald. It contains harmful substances, which are typically deadly to man and animals if either comes into contact with it. The water in the balance of the labyrinth is not fit to drink, nor is it wise to cross through it. The bottom of the watered areas contain a liquid quagmire, which swallows up everything that places its trust in it.

The only way to traverse is on very narrow strips of elevated land, sometimes only inches above the watery cemeteries. The raised land ranges from barely a foot wide to about seventeen feet across, which means it must be negotiated on foot. Almost all trails dead-end in the bogs. It is thought only one or two paths lead the entire way through the maze.

Almost all who enter to labyrinth are never seen again. Apparently, the Mizars have somehow found a way to bridge the gaps between the various paths. The reconnaissance teams that have been sent out from Kilrek to find a way through have never had success, and some never made it back at all. The task is doubly dangerous because it is thought the Mizars have a constant presence in the bogs to make sure no one makes it out alive.

As Jovar contemplates his approach to the challenge of the labyrinth and the dismal results from those have attempted this gauntlet and failed, he begins to rethink his strategy.

"Are there other ways to accomplish this?"

Not having a ready answer, it seems wise to stop for a while and consider any possible options before committing himself to a specific plan.

As he begins to see more clearly, he realizes a major road ahead is pointing north. He guides Dohar left at the junction and begins to look for a place to rest and think.

"It would be nice to come across an orchard or two," he muses.

Occasionally, there are wild orchards established by the winds, a tree here and two over there.

Within forty-five minutes, he spies one such grove about thirty yards off to the left. Within a few moments, his keen eyesight rewards him—five mature *alisorn* bushes, who thankfully bear their offerings in early summer. This is a happy find. Jovar picks as many as will fit in one of his carrying bags. The shells are relatively easy to crack, but they will remain good to eat for several months.

Jovar sits at the base of a larger tree, consuming a handful of the berries one at a time. With some assurance of keeping starvation at bay for the near future, he begins to examine his options. What does he know for certain about what he's been told over the years about the labyrinth? Almost nothing. Could he simply keep just within the labyrinth, say a few hundred yards, and stay relatively safe? Maybe. Should he leave Dohar behind and walk on foot? Not unless he absolutely has to. That would be almost certain death.

What if he meets up with a Mizar in the labyrinth? Try to take him captive, but if a struggle ensues, kill him before he kills you. What if there are large numbers of Mizars? Hide as quickly as possible. Jovar has trained Dohar to lie on his side quietly, anticipating that someday he might need to hide his horse as well as himself.

The more he reflects, the more he realizes that repeating what everyone has been doing in the past hasn't worked, so that is not a rational option. Perhaps staying within the labyrinth without charging in may be the most likely approach to staying alive the longest. There is a beginning of the labyrinth, and there must be an end. Jovar tentatively decides to stay just within the eastern fringe of the maze and see where it leads him. He will enter the maze as planned and adapt as needed.

Determining to stay just out of sight from the road until reaching the labyrinth and realizing that changing clothes would be a wise option, considering he is literally a marked man, he begins to look for an opportunity to do just that. The uniform will be kept and put on again after returning with his branch. Now he is very thankful for the gold coins hidden inside pockets of his riding boots long ago, reserved for an unforeseen emergency.

This certainly qualified. The fangore, it turns out, don't search your person, just examine your external appearance and the personals stored in the two travel

bags on the back of the saddle. Because gold is the common currency between the kingdoms, he will just wait until the opportunity arises to purchase a new set of attire. There are always people ready to receive money without asking any questions. Jovar estimates that it will take about eight days to reach the edge of the Dark Emerald—time enough to plod and plan.

UNTANGLING ROOTS

The unmarked maze becomes more difficult to accurately traverse as the twelfth day lingers on. *How far into the labyrinth am I? Are we going too far in? Will I ever come out again?*

Jovar had managed to buy some clothes from one of the travelers he met while still close to the main road. Sure enough, no questions were asked. *"As gold speaks, it often encourages silence in others."*

But now food and water is also becoming an issue for both. A few dozen berries remain, along with the original supply granted. Dohar is clearly losing weight, but most of the grass is still recognizable and can be eaten. A day and a half since fresh water was available is a serious issue, but Jovar feels compelled in some strange way to stay the course he is on. It's almost as though an invisible road is being somehow laid out before him.

Although vision is limited to several dozen yards, Jovar realizes that the ground is suddenly rising fast before them. It might be advantageous to follow the incline and perhaps climb a tree or some outcropping of rocks to get some sense as to where he might be in this predicament. A few minutes later, the undergrowth clears somewhat, and Jovar's eyes are drawn to something that is out of place in the distance.

Even though it is covered in vines, brush, and other vegetation, he can see the outline of some sort of building. His eyes become transfixed on this mirage as he comes nearer. Examining the shape, it is obviously a striking composition. Within several more minutes, he is standing before this long-abandoned monument made of unfamiliar stone. He ties Dohar to one of the trees in what now appears to be a courtyard and methodically begins to walk around an imposing structure, being deliberate and patient, both for his own safety and to try to absorb what he is witnessing.

The exterior design is apparently rectangular in shape, and assumes he is standing next to one of four walls. The present wall's length seems to be about one hundred and twenty yards or so; its height is beyond view to estimate because of the masses of vegetation clinging to its side and descending from above.

The roof is not visible but must be intact as well, given the angle some of the vegetation is cascading down. It is an important landmark for whoever made it. Maybe it is from one of the tribes that exist in the kingdoms. But if so, why would it have been abandoned? Perhaps it is a testimony of some tribe that existed eons ago. There are many questions with no answers.

As Jovar turns toward the corner to see the second face, he observes a protruding curved archway, very high and wide. It must be the entrance. Not rushing, but increasing his tempo, he hopes to get some insight into this mystery. Now standing about twenty-five feet away, centered on the entrance to appreciate its construction, his eyes are drawn to the top of the arc.

It appears to have writings or symbols on each arch stone, engraved by long-forgotten craftsmen, still announcing its message to all who would pass through the entry.

Trying to make some sense out of the mostly hidden communication, his eyes examine the left portion of the arch. Suddenly he sees partially revealed letters between the vines on the thirteenth stone. The letters are surely Umsnil. Unable to fully comprehend what he is seeing, he literally feels as though he has been struck again by a Sorek's glancing blow.

Unbelievable. How could this be possible? Why have I never heard of this in the histories of Buovonta? It has to be connected to Buovonta or the kingdoms because the language is our own tongue. His mind tries to catch up with his eyes.

Slowly retreating to the former courtyard into the longer growth, he bends a young tree over to sit on and tries to regain his composure. *How could such a thing be possible? Why would it be in the labyrinth of all places? I would never have believed this even if Zalin would have told me she had seen such a place with her own eyes.*

His mind flashes suddenly to the six who came back alive from the labyrinth.

What if they also found this place and told the authorities about it? They would have thought them to be insane, wouldn't they? Sometimes telling the truth is seen as insanity. Is it possible that Wisgraf knows about this but doesn't want to end up in Lashsborg?

Being staggered by such a revelation, he must find out what those covered words say.

Standing up and advancing to Dohar, he looks at his companion with a partial smile and shakes his head. "Well, girl, I didn't know what to expect in the labyrinth, but it certainly wasn't this."

He reaches into his measured storehouse and takes fifteen more berries to give him more strength. He must climb the arch and reveal the concealed, muted truth.

The arch is constructed out of quarried stone, each about four feet square with approximately seven feet extending out from the point where the arch and the wall meet. There are no supporting posts to sustain the overhang, so the stones must be quite long on the interior of the structure. However, the architectural design makes it very easy and safe to climb. The recessed mortar between the stones is an adequate width to accommodate a secure foot and handhold.

As Johar proceeds, he cuts away all the vegetation engulfing each stone. He is thankful weapons of war also can be used for peaceful purposes.

He decides, wisely so, not to try to decipher any statements until he completes his task on both sides of the arch.

After coming down from the second half of the arch, mission completed, he looks up at the newly revealed history. There are seemingly many other languages represented, which are inscribed on them. Each arch stone has a different type of lettering emblazoned on it. There were twenty-nine stones in all. The third stone from the apex of the arch is written in Umsnil. Although the form was not current, it's still recognizable to Jovar.

ᏯᏌᎦ ᏯᏋ ᏯᏁᏚ ᎷᏂᏁᎩ
ᏯᏌᎦ ᏯᏋ ᎷᏂᏁᎩ ᏯᏁᏚ

Jovar reads the words in a self-instructive manner, "Out of one, many. Out of many, one."

Certainly cryptic. Given the fact that each stone is written in a different script, it seems logical to Jovar that dissimilar tribes are somehow connected. It also seems rational to conclude that this is some kind of meeting place. It would be consistent if it is its original function; all of the various clans would have met here. But there are only eight kingdoms, nine counting Sorek, not twenty-nine.

His mind continues to wonder, *How could this be? The eight kingdoms speak Pefghal, the common diplomatic language of the confederation. Twenty missing tribes somewhere?*

The revelation gleaned from the facade makes it imperative to enter the building. It now is clear that at one time every tribe met in peace and lived in harmony with one another. What could have happened to dissolve so precious a union? Perhaps there would be some clues to their ability to flourish together. If so, he would be the first to apply their wisdom in his own life. There are no doors to attempt to open. They have long since rotted away. There are only four very ornate hinges on each side of the archway, about twelve feet inside the arch, which at first glance seem to be made of an unfamiliar metal. On closer examination, only a few fragments of the original doors are left, still clinging to the large rods that once held them in place. Although it is a cloudless day and very bright, not to mention hot and humid, it is very difficult to see inside the structure from where he stands. Beyond that fact, *"only fools run swiftly into ignorance."*

After a few minutes, Jovar decides to stay for the remainder of the day and to enter the mysterious interior in the morning. In the meantime, he would scour on foot in the general vicinity to investigate if any water or food are present. It seems prudent as well to examine the exterior of the structure more closely. Perhaps there may be windows higher on the walls hidden by the overgrowth. That would prove very useful in an investigation of the interior.

STRATEGY OF DECEPTION

Madnak has convened a leadership meeting. This time the *ackbisk* were gathered together. Their collective input may flesh out a plan he was beginning to formulate.

The prince outlines the purpose for the meeting and the rationale behind it. "Overcoming superior strength through exploiting perceived military weakness has never succeeded. The point of the spear was to pierce their shields, not their pride. Subtly attacking their overwhelming obsession with freeing so-called captives could be the flaw in their defenses that hopefully would prove fatal. To draw them into the assumption that we have finally come to the determination that our beliefs and way of life are defective." Ackbisk Qrudak asks the obvious question, "How would we begin this deception?"

The prince, who rarely smiles, grins in confident satisfaction. "The first step would be to convey the sign of negotiation, hoisting the tricolored flag of peace. We know the Mizars secretly position themselves out of our sight on the day of their attack, waiting for the blackness to descend. We would send one of our longest-held prisoners to go on the plain with the flag of peace, dressed in his Sorek uniform on every fully overcast day. He would be our first negotiator. If they sent one of their own to investigate, the prisoner would be able to truthfully say that we have not harmed him at all, nor forcefully interrogated him, and have treated him with great respect.

"If he is successful, we would then request through him ambassadorial meetings to find common ground, complete with suggested prisoner exchanges. Then extend an invitation to visit each other's fortresses. This process may take several years to complete. At some future date, there would be enough intelligence gathered to plan a secret attack, decisively strike when they've lowered their defenses, believing that their campaigns have finally and fully accomplished their objectives."

Ackbisk Gazium rhetorically asks, "How can you be certain they will follow so easily? Dealing with wild animals in quite unpredictable."

The prince retorts, "I am sure they are absolutely committed to either changing us or killing us. All we have to do is let them believe we now prefer to be changed rather than killed. No one has to chase a prey that has been killed. If we convince them that our change of heart is genuine, we will eventually be victorious over them."

"What if the Mizars don't come out to meet the prisoner?" Ackbisk Eggirond queries.

The prince responds without hesitation, "In that case, we will instruct the prisoner to go back to Sorek."

"Won't that give the enemy information that we don't want them to have?" Eggirond inquires.

"What information does he have that matters? When they question him, they will find out exactly what we want them to. They will obviously be surprised, first of all that he's alive and, secondly that he was treated extremely well. That will plant a seed of respect in them for us, regardless of what they have previously imagined us to be."

"That is brilliant," Ackbisk Arginsol blurts out, almost shouting.

As the prince observes the rest of the ackbisks, he sees in many faces a tacit acknowledgment of Ackbisk Arginsol's statement. The prince speaks again, "Are there any objections to this basic plan of action?"

All those seated know what that question means. That was the end of the discussion. All remain silent.

"Very well. We will continue to work on specifics, but we will begin to put this strategy into effect as soon as possible." The prince dismisses the ackbisks to the large banquet hall where they will eat and drink their fill before returning to their assigned posts.

Madnak knows the next step in the plan. He will request the other seven princes of the kingdoms to assemble at Kilrek. He will also request that at least one of the Azilium of Meyungulas to attend as well. The three Azilium are chosen strictly by the female population for their superior intelligence, physical prowess, and distinct beauty. They rule in concert and each one's tenure is granted until the age of forty, when it has been decided that they have reached the apex of their abilities. The women's ages are diverse, so there is only one replacement every several years. There has not been a strategy session among them for many years. But this meeting will be not like the others. Madnak is

confident the other princes will be just as impressed as the ackbisks were. It is too inviting not to attempt it.

His mind reflects on the other reality of their arrangement, *Kingdoms without kings. Sounds antithetical.* However, it has been long recognized that there are seven other kingdoms for a reason. Even though there are plenty of areas of agreement and mutual customs and forms such as language, there are also sharp disparities. How each kingdom is organized and functions varies, sometimes greatly between the kingdoms. Priorities within each also differ. None of the other kingdoms would have the others to rule over them. Princes are sufficient. Kingdoms can exist without kings; in this realm, it is the rule.

The princes are elected in the seven kingdoms by the military staff from the consors to the ackbisks, although each realm has their own terminology for their military. All princes are drawn from the ranks of the ackbisk. Each ackbisk is a proven warrior and leader, a veteran of many conflicts, and one who has proven leadership among those under his command. Besides being an excelling strategist, he also must be in good standing with those with whom he leads into battle.

Unless those entrusted to carry out orders respect the one giving them, it creates an unstable situation. A secret-ballot election is held in each of the kingdoms' high chamber. The votes are cast repeatedly until an ackbisk receives eighty percent of the votes. That is a sufficient number to ensure cooperation among the officers. Treason is an immediate death sentence for the guilty party and promotion for the one who discloses the treason.

This system has the potential for corruption and vengeance, but very thorough independent investigations are held to ensure the innocent aren't burned alive for no reason. That would create its own issues of loyalty. The elections are held within a month after the prince announced his retirement or resignation. If he dies in battle or by other means, a replacement is chosen within two weeks. If, on the other hand, a prince is found to be treasonous, he is publicly drawn and quartered.

Madnak has been a prince for nineteen years. Although not able to move as well when younger, he still possesses relatively good health. Those around him simultaneously respect and fear him. His eyes are continually fixed on the mission, and he does not tolerate laxness in himself or those around him. He has no intention of resigning his office or retiring until his heart's mission is completed—annihilating the Mizars. When that is accomplished, revenge will be exacted, and his life's ambition will also be complete. Fully confident in his plan, he quickly dispenses the *zagins* to deliver the invitations to the various kingdoms to meet for a strategy session.

THE EMERGING CHRYSALIS

As the procession to the common destination enters its second day, the weather welcomes all to a beautiful travel. The light breeze keeps the heat at tolerable levels, and the scenery, although familiar, has a breath of freshness about it. Because there are four distinct seasons, each provides a new perspective on the ever-changing landscape unfolding before them.

Zalin thoroughly enjoys springtime the most, when the buds begin their marvelous, unveiling of color and repetitive destiny. Summer days also have their place in her heart, but the emerging new life is a mute assurance to her that that she too is part of the cycle of the blossoming pages of her life. Just as the buds emerge from day to day, they only slightly resemble the pattern they will display when fully mature. Zalin clearly feels in the middle of an emotional metamorphosis, not enjoying the present form but knowing hidden in the recesses of her soul that the present is not the future form their lives will take.

As the group enters a xilon, the young girls are eagerly awaiting the next interaction. Ilistra is pleased she has found new playmates who view the world as she does, with imagination and adventure. Bonds are being formed easily with the trio. When the circle of experience is small, commonality abounds. The unexpected alliance comforts Zalin. Not having to be on constant guard over her emotions and field unsolicited questions from Ilistra gives welcomed relief.

Stopping for lunch this day is far more effortless than yesterday. Evonquel, apparently friendly and outgoing by nature, immediately walks toward Zalin as soon as food has been distributed to her husband and children. However, this time she is walking with the other two mothers.

"Hello, Zalin. Isn't it a superb day to travel?"

"Yes, it's simply wonderful," Zalin retorts.

Evonquel continues, "I'd like you to meet my two good friends, Javsor and Buarzel."

Both women extend their hands. All four women appear roughly the same ages, and with children, they certainly have much in common.

Zalin willingly extends her hands to reciprocate in kind, grateful there is a growing sphere of relationships rather than the solitary isolation she has been experiencing on an adult level. "Glad to meet you both," Zalin volunteers.

"Yes, likewise," they both say simultaneously, causing everyone to laugh reflexively.

Lunch in tow, they sit in a circle and begin to chat about raising children, an effortless subject for all. No need to delve in matters outside common ground. Each exchange bits of experience to which all relate. The interchange is uncomplicated and pleasant. Funny stories are intermingled with the challenges of motherhood, and the time goes by too quickly. As expected, the husbands and fathers signal lunch is over and time to proceed. There is an unspoken sense among the group of women that the newly planted seed of acquaintance may bloom into friendship before the collective journey ends.

BEAUTIFUL MEYUNGULAS

As Zagin Velmonk approaches the vale, which leads directly into the domain of the Meyungulas, lying far to the south of Buovonta, it is as if he is entering into another separate realm entirely. The vegetation seems to be bursting, rather than simply maturing. Vibrant colors slowly engulf the courier as he wades yet deeper into the now narrowing thoroughfare. Trees that he has never seen before, along with lower growing vegetation, very diverse in both content and beauty, seem to calm and mesmerize instantaneously. The overwhelming loveliness of the terrain becomes difficult to drink in and digest.

He begins to imagine how wonderful it must be to live in such a glorious environment. Becoming somewhat disorientated, he forces himself to realign with the task before him—to deliver the missive to Jelfon Omlissa, the most senior ruler of this apparent paradise.

Zagin Velmonk soon wonders why there are no obvious signs of human life as he traverses this gorgeous path. Both sides of the roadway are quite dense, and his vision cannot penetrate more than a few yards into the wooded landscape. The entire valley resembles a blanket of living paint, lavishly splashed on every part of the effervescent canvas.

The only sign of nonvegetative life are large, crimson-clad *sengens*, who glide effortlessly above him from time to time. Although they remain quite high, he is sure they are well aware of his presence. Never having seen one before, he has only been told of their hunting prowess, their expansive eight-foot wing span, and large, razor-sharp talons. Velmonk is thankful they don't seem to be showing any special interest in him. Being voracious meat eaters gives him pause, but their methodical pattern that overlaps his presence occasionally may only be coincidence.

It's important to know the difference between rational and irrational fear. Your life may depend upon it. At the present moment, Zagin Velmonk feels as if he is suspended between them. He picks up his pace ever so slightly. Running toward the unknown may prove costly.

Within forty-five minutes, the outline of the citadel abruptly appeared as the zagin negotiates around a sharp curve. The cleared fields now before him magnified the stunning sight. The imposing structure was almost glowing as a brilliant gemstone, reflecting rays of dazzling magnificence. The sight was almost beyond description, nearly magical. Whatever stone was used to construct this sculpture, it reflected and refracted light and magnified the hues with spectacular effect. It certainly conveyed the appearance of goodness and had the effect of drawing one into its charm.

Zagin Velmonk had, for a moment at least, the assumption that this sphere was beyond evil or malicious intent. Choosing to create a palate so inviting surely reflected the intent of the designer's incredible skill, who obviously appreciated and promoted loveliness. Within a few moments of sighting this dazzling edifice, there abruptly appeared a small host of sentries rapidly moving in sync toward him. Within a few more moments, they directly flanked him.

He had been informed before leaving that the Meyungulas were primarily female. But until he saw them with his own eyes, he didn't fully appreciate the descriptions given to him. The fourteen women in the enclosed circle were all tall and noticeably muscular. Each was well armed and quite beautiful and gave the clear indication that they were prepared to handle any situation that presented itself.

Zagin Velmonk slowly reached into the soft, leather pouch, retrieving the message for Jelfon Omlissa, which had already been translated into their native Yihami tongue, and handed it to the warrior in directly front of him. Although Zagin Velmonk didn't speak their language, he felt relatively certain that they wouldn't kill an unarmed messenger.

Their reputation of being fierce warriors seemed to be verified by the scene that had unfolded before him, but only the Mizars were known to have killed such emissaries. The recipient of the letter briefly glanced at the sealed velum cylinder. Noticing the recipient's name, she spoke a command to the contingent, and all instantly prepared to march forward.

Velmonk was briskly escorted up to and through the stone-slab gates that also had the iridescent quality of the balance of the complex. Once inside, he saw

many men and women actively working and talking, not really paying much attention to the entourage passing by them. Many children were also present, most playing games and enjoying the innocent life they presently possessed. They entered a massive archway and begin to climb a winding staircase that appeared to glow with a reddish tinge, not dissimilar to that of the sengens that had circled him earlier. That oddity elicited an eerie and unsettling sensation within his spirit. That similarity couldn't be a coincidence. Perhaps there was a connection that went beyond merely a symbolic gesture.

As he enters the circular edifice, his eyes are immediately drawn both to the bluish pillars that formed a simple yet elegant semicircle surrounding a large, elevated section and to the three striking women sitting on graceful white-and-amber thrones awaiting his arrival.

After being guided to stand directly before the trio of imposing women, the one seated immediately to his left asks Zagin Velmonk in flawless Umsnil, "What is the purpose of your visit?"

Not being knowledgeable of the reason of his visit, the answer was a simple one. "I was not informed of the purpose of my visit. It is the policy of Buovonta not to divulge the contents of the message to the messenger."

As he spoke, the three women were looking intently into his eyes to detect any hint of deception or dishonesty in his words. "*Truth is clarity of soul.*" Seeing no obvious signs of a ploy, they dismiss him from the room without any further inquiries.

THE QYISILINKS

The openness of the wide and relatively flat stretch of fertile terrain rapidly transforms into sparsely populated and diminished vegetation. Within a brief span, Zagin Visnon begins the physical descent into the extreme southwestern edge of the remotest kingdom. Although he perceives no one, he is well aware that *bexalars* are watching him from a variety of concealed roosts.

The craggy outcroppings that now dominate the scene before him has a slit of an opening that can only be perceived as one approaches at precisely the correct angle. Although the gap is wide enough for about twelve mounted bexalars to easily ride alongside each other, the sheer face of the stony, dark corridors seems to imperceptivity squeeze any traveler as they slowly wind every deeper into the shadows.

The downward spiral is unrelenting until no natural light penetrates the ever- descending subterranean abyss, now completely shrouded and capped with an impenetrable yet iridescent stone ceiling, which produces an eerie pale-yellowish glow. The ever-present winds create a myriad of sounds that unsettle and produce a universal sense of oppression and dread the deeper one unfamiliar with the somber realm traverses.

The dominion of the Qyisilinks is rife with real and imagined risk.

But precisely as the light behind the traveler dramatically fades, the smoothed thoroughfare ahead begins to reflect a hint of brightness. The ground gradually and increasingly emits light from some internal source, almost drawing one to itself, and produces an inner relief of not being swallowed whole by the inanimate stone sarcophagus.

Within several minutes, the scene dramatically transforms into a wide expanse of now-blinding light, revealing the heart of this peculiar domain. Tilled land and buildings cover the vast plain beyond the horizon. Although the impenetrable stone walls remain as both a hedge and voluntary prison, they have suddenly receded in the distance.

As Zagin Visnon fully emerges from the granite channel, he is immediately surrounded by well-armed bexalars, two on either side, four spaced evenly in front of him, and four behind him, who must have been following him the entire time without his knowledge.

With flawless Pefghal, a tall bexalar, standing directly in front of the zagin, calmly orders him to follow them into the sanctuary, an imposing structure perhaps four hundred *spliks* away. The contrast of scenery and company was starkly antithetical. Rather than a host of stealth shadows lurking in wait to attack, the demeanor and disposition of his escorts are practically congenial. Although physically fit and obviously capable of wielding what they carry, there is no hint of either desiring to instill fear or intimidation upon their charge. A solemn yet peaceful demeanor permeates the entourage.

Crossing through the unusual circular massive gates, apparently fully opened for internal commerce and other such interchanges within the kingdom, the scene remains uninterrupted. The randomly assembled residents are unmoved to the point of not even glancing at the subject of the cadenced train. Zagin Visnon quietly wonders whether this sight is a daily occurrence, which would seem unlikely given the dread nature of the initial entry.

Several minutes pass before they arrive before an imposing structure made of stone unknown to Zagin Visnon. All briefly halt and momentarily pause at the base of massive steps, each a singular, polished slab of iridescent dark green, complementing the brownish facade of the apparent residence of Segmegadim, prince of Qyisilinks.

Resuming the cadence, the group moves smoothly through the high-arched entrance into an expansive open dome. Sitting expectantly on an ivory-colored throne replete with bright-red fabric draped elegantly behind the coved structure is Prince Segmegadim.

His look is impressive in both stature and demeanor, handsome in appearance and his other physical attributes speaking for themselves. He commands an almost-reflexive respect. Zagin Visnon has the immediate impression that form and substance are complementary, not contradictory, with this leader. The human train comes to a unified halt a respectful distance from the throne.

The prince motions for the lead bexalar to approach him and inform him of the exact nature this guest is in his presence. After hearing the character of the visit, he instructs the bexalars to retrieve the missive.

Apparently reading the epistle carefully, he then looks up at Zagin Visnon and asks, "Have all the other kingdoms agreed to participate?"

The zagin could only speak for what he had been told before he left on his assignment. "Prince Segmegadim, I was sent out at the same time as the rest of the messengers and am unaware of the responses of any of the other kingdoms. Because your kingdom is the farthest away from Buovonta, I would expect that I will also be the last to be informed of the decisions of the other leaders."

"Very well. After I find out what the others have decided, I will give my response. You may convey that message to Prince Madnak."

Fully aware that the conversation has just ended, Zagin Visnon respectfully bows before the prince and asks permission to return with his message. The prince motions for him to leave with his right hand, and the assembled troops begin their journey back to where they had their initial contact.

REVITALIZING FIND

J ovar, revived by the diminishing store of berries and energized by the mystery speaking before him, begins to walk in every expanding concentric circles, keeping the outline of the inexplicable building within sight. In only a few minutes, he stumbles unto a circular rock formation, about waist high. He hopes that what he is seeing is not a delusion. As he closes in a straight line to the object, his hope is confirmed. It is a long-abandoned well, covered with overgrowth, but a well nonetheless.

He rejoices inwardly at such a wonderful discovery. He immediately begins to dismantle the diminutive jungle grasping the source of potentially fresh water. If the font is a spring or an underground stream, it will be relatively easy to clear out the debris and draw up fresh water in just a matter of hours. Not certain how deep the well is, or how he will clean out or draw the costly liquid, he concentrates on the task at hand.

After an hour and a half, as the undergrowth begins to release its grip to the sharp blade, Jovar peers into the spherical blackness. As his eyes adjust, he realizes there are too many leaves and branches covering the bottom of the well to determine if water is present. Meandering again, within eight yards he finds a stone large enough to answer the question. Releasing the twelve-pound rock at arm's length, it finds its target. The bottom suddenly explodes in a glorious splash, thankfully verifying the first theory.

Now to clear the water. He decides to use one of the leather pouches that carries his possessions. Carefully emptying the contents into the remaining storage bins, he cuts off a sturdy flexible vine on the return trip to the well. Carefully tying the vine to the leather bucket, he also fits an X-shaped branch near the surface of the bucket to enhance its opening capacity.

The first attempt proves successful. But upon examining the contents, it is clearly fouled, apparently a spring that needs to be cleansed. But persistence will yield clean water. Two hours pass quickly. The water begins to change color—first, a lighter gray brown, then a light brown. Two more hours of hard work and the water looks almost normal. He decides to wet his lips. As thirsty as he was, gulping large amounts of unclean water could prove deadly. Jovar first dips his fingers into the almost-clear water. It tastes somewhat like water containing mossy rocks, but it doesn't react with his lips or throat. He dares to take a slight palm full. This time it tastes somewhat woody as well, so he waits to see if his stomach rebels. He walks slowly back to Dohar to test his theory. Coming within about eight feet of Dohar, she whiffs deeply. Jovar knows she smells the water on his hands. He still feels normal, so he allows her to lick his still-moist hands. She is excited and desirous for more.

It will another hour of clearing the well before he and Dohar will begin to drink freely. His stomach has not yet reacted. Now he is reasonably confident the water is safe for both of them. Managing to extract all of the large branches, only a few of the smaller branches are left in the mostly cleared water. Bringing up a full-leather bucket, he pauses momentarily and then takes a longer drink. His throat seems to feel every drop of needed nourishment to his body. Briefly pausing, he feels no ill effects. It is time to bring his precious cargo to Dohar. She begins to prance in place, knowing what she is about to receive. Jovar brings the offering to her nose, and she drinks deeply, looking directly into Jovar's eyes, presenting an unblinking gaze of thanksgiving.

Evening fast approaching, Jovar decides to sleep by Dohar. Unfurling his thick blanket, placed a few feet away from his mare, he secures a makeshift pillow to lay his head and dream about where to step next. As an unlimited source of fresh water now a reality, Jovar shifts his needs stratagem. If he could find a reliable food source, he could stay in this place for a while. It will take days to cut the vegetation from the roof, enough to reveal any windows or other natural-light sources.

The other option is to venture deeper into the labyrinth to find one of the tar pits and make torches to enter the archway's unknown interior. That would be less desirable, considering the potential hazards of such a venture. Besides, leaving Dohar for several days was a chance he didn't want to take. For the immediate future, the odds were favorable to discover a sacred orchard, which could conceivably provide adequate food for weeks or months. Fresh from the water discovery, Jovar's confidence grows that such a traditional grove would be in the vicinity. So far, he hasn't come across any of the dangerous animals he had heard about.

INTERNAL DREVKREZ

The farthest northwestern kingdom's topography was rugged and very difficult terrain to negotiate with many large rock outcroppings, blind canyons, including some treacherous wildlife sprinkled among the dense forests. The weather was often unpredictable and, at times, life threatening. Yet the Drevkrez kingdom and its inhabitants were perfectly suited for each other. A visually arresting environment coupled with a populace equipped with a jagged demeanor produced an obscure volcano-like atmosphere of unpredictability and potential for impulsive violent eruptions. The presence of many natural physical barriers inhibited regular interchange, and nonresidents rarely knowingly traversed their lands.

The homeland was entirely self-sufficient, but they still had to be prepared for the threat of Sorek. Therefore, necessity creates many unlikely alliances. Their expertise in waging covert warfare rivaled that of the Mizars, which made them an important collaborator in the final scheme. The only persistent enemy they had to contend with was their counterparts to the southeast. Therefore, the invitation appealed to their self-interest, which was the only commodity they valued or ever negotiated in and was, in itself, an extremely rare occurrence.

Oddly enough, this kingdom did not covet other sovereignties' possessions. Perfectly content to live within their borders, the majority of clashes were internal, which often led to bloodshed. Ancient grievances regularly fueled aggressive and deadly behavior among the factions, yet any external hostility instantly ignited a unified firestorm.

Being thoroughly familiar with these realities, Zagin Gezbekel was chosen for the mission. Fluent in Suwuvil and the husband of a native of the region, he had survived several encounters. Suspicious of all outsiders, one had to be quite adept at remaining calm when a human cauldron boiled over for no apparent reason. His wife, Cosgur, revealed this tactic was occasionally a ploy designed to intimidate, implying a veiled threat of harm for any infractions. But most often, it involved an agitated and aggressive paranoid resident. Many who ventured into their lands failed to return.

As a young man, Gezbekel unknowingly crossed over the border while pursuing a wounded prey. Shortly thereafter, he stumbled onto a seriously injured Drevkrez leader who had fallen down a rocky outcropping. He quickly brought him to his village on his own mount and subsequently saved his life.

After the incident, the man insisted he marry his daughter, apparently an ancient custom of the region. Discerning that insulting anyone, let alone a leader, was almost certainly writing one's own premature death warrant, he complied. He had absolutely no interest in proving his impromptu theory. He was, in fact, grateful his daughter was attractive and approximately the same age, although clearly older than himself. They also allowed them to return to Buovonta because of his heroics, an unprecedented act of grace for this group.

He had not been back to the area for several years. He and Cosgur would bring their three children to visit her family on occasion but didn't stay more than a few days. Thankfully, Cosgur didn't apparently inherit any of the paranoia that plagued most of the kingdom and didn't pass it on to their own offspring, for which Gezbekel was very thankful.

As soon as Zagin Gezbekel came within eyesight of the citadel, he could sense from that distance the anxiety that emanated from the secured stronghold. Within a few moments, emissaries from the walls appeared, directly and swiftly approaching his position.

When the zagin came within probable earshot, he spoke firmly in the vernacular, "I am Zagin Gezbekel from Kilrek with a message for Prince Zek Wilfmelk."

The response was immediate and clear. "Stop where you are and wait until we are in your midst." Within a few more moments, the twelve-member guard surrounded him.

Although he was technically attached to this kingdom, he was very careful to keep the interchange official. If someone recognized him, so be it; otherwise, he felt it would be best not to bring any extraneous elements into the situation. This group didn't need any assistance in arousing any residual suspicion that may be lurking within the column.

He and his wife and three children had briefly visited Cosgur's family about four years earlier, but they knew that extended stays weren't emotionally healthy for any of them, especially their children. They had apparently escaped the inherited tendencies, but neither parent wanted any influence to linger any longer than absolutely necessary. Even Cosgur's parents seem to have a tacit understanding of what was best for their own grandchildren and cooperated with the succinct appointments.

Once passing through the gates into the expansive Fosmalic, the unique hub of the kingdom, the creativity of the inhabitants was obvious. Although a fair distance from the front gates, the prince's residential facade was impressive. Four natural purplish stone sentinels rose symmetrically from the earth and surrounded a singular, massive, light-green stone that was somewhat cylindrical in shape. Although all of the rock was natural, it was inconceivable that this formation had naturally materialized in its present form.

Inserted into the sides of the four stones and hewn into the central configuration were intensely white slab steps, which rose gracefully and concluded at the apex of the structure that housed the ruling contingent. The palace was somewhat compact but built with a bluish- and white-laced material that seemed to blend in and proceed from the green pedestal it was perched on despite its obvious contrast.

Walking up the staircase gave the neophyte zagin the feel that he was about to enter a royal presence, which the kingdoms officially rejected. However, the external trappings of an elevated leader were abundantly displayed in all the realms. Those who

ruled served as the consent of the masses, which was as firm a principle as the steps he was treading on, but there was no hesitation to display grandeur fitting for royalty nonetheless.

Entering the elaborate main hall, still flanked by his dozen escorts, Zagin Gezbekel methodically proceeds toward the throne until ordered to halt. He stood a discerning distance from whom he supposed was Prince Zek Wilfmelk, who was seated in a robust dark-green throne. A well-armed man proceeds from the left side of the throne to retrieve the message from the messenger. An aide to the prince's right examines the document, quietly sharing its contents with the prince. Without any discernable expression or comment, the prince gestures for the twelve to escort the courier out of his presence. Within a few minutes, his mission accomplished, Zagin Gezbekel begins the journey back to Kilrek.

EZTROBEL

Overlooking the Wild Sea, Eztrobel has impressive natural defenses similar to Sorek. It has a secure, liquid northern border and also stands as a beacon, constructed on 250-foot cliffs that jut out of the land just yards from the sea, not enough room for the enemy to assemble in any large numbers. Hurling even smaller stones would prove to be deadly for anyone on the ground below. Attack by any vessels on the sea would leave them exposed to a massive barrage of fire and stone. Therefore, it is only necessary to assign several *swomtig* to warn with their *juxul*'s horns of any potential attack, leaving the bulk of the guardians free to reinforce the three remaining walls.

The north wall is the highest, with the east and west walls cascading unevenly down the gradual slope of the cliffs until they reach the lowest point to join with the southern wall, thirty-two feet above the surrounding countryside. The platform to allow access and exit on the south entry is lowered by massive chains. Identical materials of Buovonta jankel wood fully encased by kakinza protect the gate.

Although they reside on a massive amount of stone, the cliffs are very resistant to being quarried, splitting into irregular shapes and often shattering in

| D. Michael Carriere

the process. Therefore the buildings within the fortress are an interesting mix of architectural design, utilizing the materials of usable stone with dimensional beams. Because of this defect, the exterior walls are a mixture of rock and beams. The beams on the outside walls are also sheathed with kakinza, which make an interesting visual kaleidoscope, certainly not ideal but still formidable to anyone attempting to breach their defenses.

The weapons of choice are the long-shafted arrows with exceedingly sharp blades. Having perfected a five-bladed head perfectly balanced with the shaft gives greater accuracy and length as it tracks toward its intended target. The shafts are made of *vsirun*, a flexible yet very strong and straight grained wood, which permits a true flight path. Piercing light armor and incorporating small spikelike claws on the shaft just beyond the head makes it very difficult to retract the arrow from its victim once it contacts flesh or bone.

In addition, the swomtigs have devised a deadly sling that dispenses a star-shaped device that also slices into any exposed flesh it assaults. As with the arrows, this too has barbs curving outward, making retrieval of the device next to impossible without removing additional flesh in the process. The star is not intended to immediately kill its victim, although that does occur, but rather leave the wound subject to infection, and often gangrene or some other invisible menace delivers the final blow.

Their prince, Yexilpar, a crafty survivor of scores of conflicts, is one of the finest archers Eztrobel has had in their long history. A favorite among the *brugons*, as well

| 98

as the *leviks* and swomtigs, for his heroism in desperate battles, he almost rises to the level of divinity.

Despite a massive scar that runs diagonally across his face—from his left forehead, over his nose, and concludes at the bottom of his right jaw—his appearance enhances, not detracts from, his stature. No one in the kingdom is more well known than Yexilpar, and no one can claim more kills than he.

Although his fame is unmatched in the kingdom, despite his obvious appearance as a warrior, he is in fact, a very humble man about his accomplishments—a rare prince indeed. He also has three young boys, all in training for combat. Although one might expect a demand from their father to excel as he has, he applies no pressure on them except to do their best and use their natural giftedness. If they become accomplished warriors on the battlefield, so be it. If, however, they are tacticians or craftsmen in developing other effective weapons, it doesn't matter. His only request is for them to be faithful to their calling, which they are. He is truly a gentleman who is as proficient at killing his enemy as any who has every walked on their soil.

The monthly strategy session among Eztrobel's military elite is both respectful and vibrant. They meet at Klimpend, the village designated as the military headquarters. The brugons don't hesitate to give their opinions on every subject and are encouraged to do so. Experience has shown Prince Yexilpar that revelation is not the sole possession of any one individual, regardless of rank, and may come from any quarter. Therefore, he often asks questions of leviks and swomtigs for their

opinion on any matter that interests him as well as them. The "shooting star" was one such innovation that originated from a swomtig who wanted to devise a simple way to incapacitate the enemy. It has proved to be a scourge to their adversaries.

At the moment, the subject at hand is how to best ambush an approaching force before they come within ten miles of Eztrobel.

The leading proponent of a limited-casualty approach is Brugon Vurhexim. "First, send out *lewaqinks* into all of the possible routes to Eztrobel. When they discover an approaching enemy, they will quickly ride back to alert us. We then dispatch three times the estimated number of our troops toward them. However, we deploy one-third of our troops on either side of the route, about one-quarter-mile away from the route, and send the remaining one-third to confront the enemy. We will mount an offensive but quickly retreat because of being badly outnumbered. The enemy will smell blood and pursue our troops. When in the right position, a swomtig will sound the alarm with the juxul, and we will flank them and block their retreat and overpower their forces completely."

This approach has worked in the past, but only when used sparingly. Yexilpar orders a *qinsab* to search the records of war to determine the last attempt and results of a similar campaign.

The next to speak is Brugon Drazmigon, one of Yexilpar's closest advisors. They have fought together for over three decades and were both brugons until Yexilpar was recently promoted. "I believe we need to cause diversionary tactics and split the enemy into four easy pieces. We will wait until they have been en route for three days. We will then send a *lewaqink*, dressed as their own messenger, to approach them from the rear and tell them they are being attacked by another kingdom and request sending back as many troops as possible. They will certainly send some and will easily be defeated by ambush. We then allow the balance of the force to proceed another day, and we will then blow the juxuls from three different positions, forcing the commanders to split their forces, and we will overrun them with vastly superior numbers."

Yexilpar has been on similarly successful missions before over the years. This too is to be analyzed by the historians. The interchanges continue for another hour and a half until the qinsab's report. Both of the previously attempted tactics worked successfully. The second option resulted in fewer casualties, and it hadn't been attempted for several decades.

After further discussions of the proposals, the brugons agree they would like to pursue Drazmigon's approach within two months, to take advantage of favorable weather conditions. Yexilpar agrees with their evaluation and will meet with six of the senior brugons the following week. He dismisses the commanders and returns to his home, high on the cliffs. His residence overlooks the vast Wild Sea, perched high above the bluish waters as a type of *okwillian*, constantly peering with sharp vision for a prey to devour.

THE GROVE

Morning's light awakens Jovar, introducing him to a fully lighted expedition. His spirits revived from the newly discovered well, he arises quickly and continues the methodical search for food. The grove would have been planted in an open field, affording plenty of sunlight. The fact that the courtyard is still recognizable also bodes well for a find. It was probably planted on the southern part of the knoll to take advantage of the daylight.

Beginning where he finished the day before, Jovar moves systematically as a leader of men would instinctively do, making clockwise concentric circles, expanding the circles approximately twenty yards for each completed round. Before initiating the next sweep, he inscribes a large mark with his knife on a tree, forming a straight visual line from the previous loop that leads, tree by inscribed tree, directly back to the supposed temple.

After several hours of a semicircle reconnaissance, as he anticipated, the tangled jumble begins to open up. Sensing that this may be what he's been searching for, Jovar stops and peers southward. His keen observational skills detect rows of growth about forty yards farther down the knoll. Carefully marking his departure points, he begins to be rewarded.

Another twenty yards bear the second significant life-giving discovery—a mature occinal orchard of perhaps seventy-five trees. Almost all are producing their wonderful fruit. Because they ripen over several months, even the immature fruit is suitable for eating, even though it is more bitter than sweet. *"Hunger ignores perfection."*

Jovar reaches out and plucks one of the more ripened orbs and slowly bites into its firm exterior. As expected, it is somewhat bitter and hard, but still edible.

With both water and food in abundance at arm's length, Jovar begins to consider his need to immediately pursue the ligith branch given his sudden fortunes. There is no longer the necessity to rush toward his goal at the expense that haste brings. His curiosity is thoroughly piqued at the abandoned temple grounds; he is now committed, not merely for his own satisfaction but also for the kingdom's sake, to investigate the matter more expansively.

There is no telling what will be articulated as the structure speaks its muted sign language. His archeological work may unravel and reveal a key to the past that may have application for the present. Pausing for a few more moments to capture his thoughts, he slowly begins to walk through the surprisingly well-preserved outdoor sanctuary that has granted him yet another stay of execution. Only gathering the ripest offerings presented to him, another hour passes. His clothing doubling as pouches, he secures sufficient

stores for a week or so. *Time to retrace the marked path to share yet more good news with Dohar*, Jovar thought.

After sharing his bounty with his companion, he again plots the course to proceed. Having time as an ally rather than an adversary alters the threshold of necessity to one of convenience. Now it appears that clearing the roof of the sanctuary from debris and aggressive growth would offer the best and safest avenue to reveal the inner repository of an archaic past. Surely it is not just a rudimentary period that needs to be revealed, but his own ancestors' fingerprints. The plethora of other inhabitants also entombed in this crypt hint of blood and social relationships that will inescapably be traced back to a common bond, the significance of which is astounding to imagine. The internment of revelation encased in this forgotten headstone has implications well beyond anyone's present capacity to believe or accept. *"But truth is its own best interpreter."*

Jovar's inner reservoir is quickly gathering additional resolve. *"Ignoring the past is to be presently deceived, which ensures future destruction."* Even though he is certain there will be more questions than answers, the few clues he has unearthed has already shown ominous markers of a path once taken that needs to be trod once again. The more that is exposed, the closer the respective societies are to their own resurrection. Stumbling into destiny is to fortunately trip into one's own future.

Yet there is much to accomplish for him and Dohar before the day is spent, and evening is fast advancing. After leading her to the best grasses, carrying sufficient water, and consuming another personal meal from the newly discovered storehouse, evening was nigh. Johar lays down once again near his faithful companion, filled with delight at such providential events. Dreams of his family as well as imagining the significance of the partially identified unknowns, whose veil has already begun to slowly slip to the side, will likely consume the evening musings.

For one unaccustomed to experiencing such epic and dramatic illumination, the rapid unfolding of a tapestry of countless years stretches and compresses time simultaneously. Incredibly, only a few days have transpired, yet Jovar's understanding has likely traveled centuries within a fraction of the labyrinth.

Rather than facing imminent death, which yet may happen, a comet—like revelation from a configuration of stones, is declaring that a peaceful life may be about to begin anew—not just for him and his family but also for all who will embrace the truth of this testimony from the graveyard of swallowed history.

DEADLY LYBUKOM

Far to the southeast of the labyrinth lies the deceptively docile realm of the Lybukom. Although well armed with a unique form of warfare, they have no real interest in intermingling with the other kingdoms, save for occasional forays to replenish various domestic livestock. Diverse carnivorous beasts regularly reduce their source of food and primary workforce. However, if the predators get too aggressive, they will employ their chief weapon—rotted flesh saturated with a lethal concoction—which results in a very quick, gruesome, and painful death for the consumer.

For their part, the Lybukoms tend to be very careful in dispensing fatalities, being fully aware that it will stalk them if they become careless. After visually inspecting the lethal site, they will quickly burn both the deadly dose as well as the expired victims. All the kingdoms are aware of their ability to spread death, so they are thankful they choose to be responsible with their mysterious weapon. The occasional interlopers who have attempted to steal their recipe have been themselves hastily transformed into an involuntary funeral pyre, not getting far with their terminal producing product.

As Zagin Rempim approaches the denuded area surrounding the expansive and very high walls of Gevrugez, he feels relaxed, knowing that this group is almost too friendly when on their territory. They exhibit a kind of calmness, a rather casual demeanor that belies their potent arsenal. The only time they are physically armed is when they venture beyond their borders, and only with conventional weapons. However, no one is ever certain that the plague is not within arm's reach if trouble erupts. This indefinite reality causes transactions to be quite cordial, especially with the seller.

When Rempim comes within a few hundred yards of the complex, the massive doors begin to open, and he spies several members of an entourage approaching him with a distinct nonmilitary gait. Unlike Fortress Kilrek, these ambassadors appear lackadaisical, not marching but sauntering. He takes note that although the gates are quite high, they are also quite thin in contrast to Kilrek's. He concludes that they are made of *belixium*, a very straight, tenacious wood that only grows in very high altitudes.

As the two parties meet, the elder-looking man asks a simple question, "What is the purpose of your visit to us?"

Without hesitation, Rempim replies, "I come bearing an invitation from Prince Madnak of Buovonta for your prince, Pazquain."

The elder immediately motions with his hand to proceed toward the open gates. Upon entering the grounds, he notices that most of the residents acknowledge his presence and offer a slight smile. It felt

odd to the zagin that such cordiality would be shown to a total stranger, given the emotionless fortress of Kilrek.

Within a few minutes, they approached a large, polished archway facade, a smooth, light-gray stone that reflected your image as you passed by. Just beyond the entry point was a wide spiral staircase made of *ezmeniad*. The elegant stairway escorted them into an expansive hall lined with carved furniture from many exotic species of wood and stone. A slightly elevated area on the back wall featured five seated dignitaries. The central figure was apparently Prince Pazquain.

The escorted group stops within several yards of the assembled leadership. After given permission to come closer, Zagin Rempim bows slightly and reaches into his pouch to deliver the request. This letter was written in both Pefghal and Zilquani, given the fact that the two kingdoms had not met for several generations.

Prince Pazquain personally receives the letter, smiling slightly at the exchange. Zagin Rempim returns the gesture and slightly bows a second time. He retreats to his former position and awaits further instruction. The prince begins to read for a moment and then gently motions for the entire party to exit the premises. However, before they turn, the prince thanks Rempim for delivering the epistle to him. The thought enters his mind for a brief moment to request residency. However, he would be leaving behind a wife and six children, so he quickly relents of his reactive guttural response to unabashed friendliness.

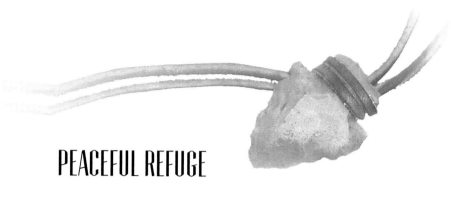

PEACEFUL REFUGE

The caravan crests a final hill to come within sight of Zwenvestin, a large village lying quietly on a broad plain. The river Nebielk, flowing from the hills, roughly divides the wooden-and-stone conclave in half. The town has four bridges to span the waterway, equally spaced to make the traversing convenient for its residents. It is a strategic gateway, connecting directly to three kingdoms, the Drevkrez, Vigpulgs, and the Qyisilinks. The trio of arteries converges into one just north of the outskirts of the settlement. It had been determined long ago that this configuration would minimize congestion and keep the village from becoming unwieldy. The topography of the rugged terrain directed the building of the roads to meet at this point. Each of the three entities has natural valleys on its southern border, which funnel travels into a bottleneck only miles from each other, making the intersection the most logical place to come together.

Within twenty minutes, the convoy comes to rest just outside the Zwenvestin proper, and the passengers disembark to stretch their limbs and to exchange final words. The quartet of girls simply continues their conversations without hesitation. The mothers swap logistical information and make plans to gather in the common courtyard to extend their relationships. This leaves time to adjust to their immediate responsibilities of resettling and organizing their households once again.

Evonquel, the unofficial leader of the group, makes the final suggestions. "Let's meet in the courtyard at three p.m. on Saturday, ten days from today. We can meet for an hour or so and talk about how to get together at one another's homes from time to time."

Javsor, Buarzel, and Zalin nod in approval.

Zalin interjects, "As you know, I'm visiting my mother, so I will have to ask her if she wouldn't mind if we meet in her house."

The quartet nods in assent. The impromptu meeting draws to a close with a light touch of hands, not too aggressive yet not without feeling or meaning.

Zalin nudges Salib to continue in the same direction. After the third bridge, Zalin guides the horse into a right turn. They continue down the road until they exit the rows of homes and travel another seven miles. Finally, they come to an intersection that branches left. The ground is now leading gently, but steadily, upward. Another mile and a half is traveled until they come to a narrow pass. Turning left again, they rise for several hundred yards and then begin to slowly descend. Salib continues his steady plod, assumingly knowing the way, as he has traversed this ground many times before. The steady breeze keeps him cool, as well as fill all their nostrils with the pleasant scent of a growing and maturing plethora of plants and grains. The fields surrounding the trio reflect the multihued glory of colors.

As they top the crest of the hill, Ilistra blurts out, "There it is."

Zalin's childhood home nestles as a precious jewel in her heart. The countless memories and wonderful times spent with her parents and Filoquaid remain etched in her soul forever. Even the pain she suddenly experiences thinking about her father doesn't diminish the good times spent and lived here.

Both also see, at the same time, Nesigil tending to her beloved flower garden. She is kneeling, busily tending to her charges, but facing away from them, not immediately realizing their presence. But the squeal of delight by her granddaughter alerts her of them. She quickly turns her head toward the young admirer's expression of deep love and anticipation. A surprised smile covers her delighted face. Nesigil quickly rises up and walks toward the gate, which grants entry into their yard and home. As Salib comes to an anticipated stop, Zalin and Ilistra quickly get off their wagon, and the three embrace on the narrow lane in front of the gate.

"I can hardly believe I'm seeing you both. What a wonderful surprise. I'm assuming Jovar is off for a longer assignment."

Zalin looks at her mother with a less-than-vibrant smile and simply looks at her without speaking. Briefly forgetting what Ilistra believes to be true, Zalin quickly recovers with a false fact.

"Yes, he's gone for a while. But he'll be back soon."

Her mother knows her daughter well enough to sense that her statement wasn't quite right. She immediately suspects something might be wrong but pretends she

didn't catch the inconsistency in her daughter's words and face.

"Well then, let's get your belongings into your rooms."

Zalin reaches back into the wagon and hands Ilistra her bundle and then grasps hers. The reunited threesome turns together and strides toward the house. There will be much to talk about.

THE CYVEH OF FRUWMUNJIE

Far to the southeast lies the Fruwmunjie. Having been forewarned by his immediate superior, the zagin proceeds cautiously around the final bend of the well-maintained thoroughfare. The solbon is gliding slowly down near the horizon. As his vision fastens on his destination, it causes an unusual reaction—fear mingled with awe. *"To see with our eyes jerks our imagination to earth."* The expansive *brvistin* stronghold stands before him like a dark, glowing jewel, forbidding yet mesmerizing. Although lifeless, it seems to practically dare one to challenge it. He slowly brings Rytop to a full stop in front of the posts and secures her next to the dark-red *vesmor* outcropping. The Pefghal commands are quite clear, engraved prominently on the bloody stone: "Walk briskly toward the citadel without surveying the surroundings."

Shadowy sentries peer down unseen from their secluded and secure perch to observe Prince Madnak's zagin approaching with measured caution. Although relations between the various tribes are marginally friendly, not being in regular contact for extended periods of time gives Zagin Gex a heightened sense of insecurity. Knowing the particular penchant of the Fruwmunjie to dispatch trespassers with lightning velocity makes advancement a very unpleasant experience. Even with the symbolic fedora worn prominently on his skull doesn't diminish the apprehension.

Without warning, the zagin is instantaneously surrounded by four heavily armed Cyveh. Beads of cool sweat abruptly begin oozing from his stunned forehead, his heart having already tumbled headlong unto his feet. No one is smiling. Zagin Gex begins to utter swift speech in Pefghal. Unable to disguise his intense fear, he succinctly reports the purpose of his presence. Without verbally responding, the overtly muscular warrior in front of him motions to walk toward the Fruwmunjie's foreboding fortress, glistening in the distance, only minutes away. Momentarily relieved that he still has breath to draw, he numbly matches the cadence with the lethal entourage.

Entering through two massive *krespind* gates, those guarding the entrance cast lengthy, judgmental glares at the foreigner. Friendliness is apparently not a part of their inherited traits. If there was not a common enemy, Zagin Gex doubts he would still be alive, or at least not alive and pain free. The coldness of the place is readily palatable if not digestible.

The messenger is presently ushered into a spherical building, complete with three apparent interrogators. His escorts remain within easy striking distance in case he would attempt anything remotely suggesting aggressiveness. Thankfully, he is not insane himself. They motion for the epistle, which he quickly retrieves. After the trio is finished reading the invitation, they dismissively gesture for the armed band to remove the zagin from the premises. Praying they would bring him back to the entrance, he begins to cautiously and silently rejoice as they return to the menacing-looking gates. Another wave of the muscular one's left hand, and Zagin Gex is released.

Enormously relieved to be freed, he smartly exits the bizarre grounds, not daring to look back nor increase his pace, lest they change their minds about him. During this relatively slow-motion escape, the more tempered and grateful zagin contemplates why this formidable-looking tribe had not been able to dispatch Sorek. Or why haven't they attempted to destroy the rest of the kingdoms for that matter? All the qualities necessary to mete out unlimited quantities of pandemonium and eradicate anything or anyone from their presence at will or whim are in abundant supply.

Such obvious power melded with an absence of compassion and conscience usually means prompt destruction for those unfortunate enough to be anywhere near their dens. Gratified to be alive, he doubts it had anything to do with empathy. Logic dictates expediency and self-preservation. At the moment, it doesn't matter what their motives are; he will see his family again.

LEZON BAQNS OF VIGPULGS

ZaginTrulon nervously awaits his audience with Lezon Baqns, the commander of the Vigpulgs. Flanked by two imposing, well-armed *mafgrix*, Zagin Trulon is escorted into an expansive chamber. Seated behind a stout and elaborate *xorol* table, Lezon Baqns appears to be quite tall. His stern demeanor and direct eye contact communicates internal vigilance and tacitly cautions against personal conflict with the stare's owner. Form and substance occasionally unite in an individual, and this Lezun may be an example of such a union. Reputed to have slain hundreds of various enemy opponents, it would seem logical to have this icon at the helm of a storied and physically striking clan.

Although Zagin Trulon has not been informed of the content of his epistle, it seems apparent that a meeting is being planned, given the fact that correspondence between the kingdoms is rare. As the sealed document is directly placed on the table in front of Lezun, he declines to directly pick up the missive. Motioning to one of the protectors, immediately flanking his left to open it, his eyes keep fastened on the zagin to detect any slight emotion that would suggest foul intensions.

In times past, enemies have delivered messages tainted with *vosmelic* on the pages. "Detachment invites evil to assume destiny's throne." After observing no ill effects by the intermediate contact, Lezun commences to read the note. The adage has been firmly rooted throughout the kingdoms for eons yet without producing sustainable fruit. Clearly meant to motivate, it also has the additional trait of creating despair. Lezun inhales more distinctly as the epistle continues. *"Words have substance when producing acts."* Commander Baqns finishes the page-and-a-half invitation without any other outward expression. Motioning with a slightly raised brow, the zagin is swiftly escorted out of his presence. Once removed, the order is given: "Call the *vijinct* to the battle quarters at once."

MYSTIFYING INTERIOR

J ovar begins this day with planned resolve. Although desperately wanting to see what the man-made cavern holds, it is apparent that to remove the enormous, accumulated growth encapsulating the roof will take several days. This means methodically pacing oneself to avoid exhaustion and injury. The first step is to ascertain the soundness of the roof itself. Because the outline can be clearly seen, it implies integrity, but it will need a close inspection before proceeding.

Jovar climbs one of the trees that overhang the roof. A large branch affords a bridge well onto the roof's platform. As he slowly shimmies along the wooden route, his eyes focus on the layered stone shingles, looking for any obvious defects or breeches. Seeing none, he slowly lowers himself onto the roof, first very lightly, then with more pressure, still firmly grasping the branch in case of a sudden break in the roof tiles. Finally allowing his full weight on the roof, it feels sound. Because the pitch of the roof is very gentle, it will be relatively easy to stand on and work from.

Jovar returns to retrieve his tools and slashes the first vine with his blade and cuts cleanly through it. He begins the process about fourteen feet from the edge of the roof, assuming that any windows would be inset some distance from the end wall. Once a vine is severed, Jovar untangles it from its companions and cuts into the remaining vegetation surrounding it. He then proceeds carefully to the edge of the roof to throw them over the side. He calculates that it will take approximately an hour to clear a two-foot-wide path to the roof's edge. The temple is orientated north and south, with the entryway facing south, so Jovar begins on the eastern-facing roof line to catch the morning solbon. Every two hours, Jovar descends from his perch to refresh himself with water and fruit, as well as remind Dohar that they are in this together.

After eight hours of difficult work, having cleared approximately sixteen feet of roof line, Jovar retreats again to be refreshed on the ground. As he looks up at his progress, he suddenly realizes that he has uncovered the side of a likely window, seeing the right side of the frame about twenty feet off the ground. As he approaches for closer inspection, he walks beyond his vantage point and realizes that there is indeed a window and that the opening is barely visible. Jovar smiles and briskly saunters toward the entryway to peer into the sanctuary to see if any light has penetrated the interior.

As his eyes begin to adjust to the inner sanctuary, he observes a tiny spray of indirect light illuminating a small sliver of the stone floor far off into the temple. As he strains to see any additional detail, there is a shadowy structure just brushing the light shaft, which appears to be a series of steps, although he can't be certain. A sense of satisfaction and excitement rise up in Jovar's spirits, confirming in part what he hopes to view in full several days hence.

Now knowing that windows exist, Jovar climbs back up and clears the next two-foot section within the hour. Without descending to the ground, he turns his attention to the western roof opposite the now-exposed window to allow the afternoon solbon to illume the same site, assuming that the windows would be symmetrical. As he descends after another hour or so of hard yet willing labor, he reappears at the entryway to look inside again. This time it is obvious that there are steps leading to what Jovar assumes is a large altar. The just-cleared west side of the roof does reveal light piercing through a matching, mostly covered window, revealing in more detail the imposing artifact.

The altar has four large, engraved legs, which figures why Jovar can't decipher where he stands. The legs are approximately four feet high, forming the base for a hefty and thick, smooth slab of stone, which extends approximately four feet beyond the legs in each direction. On top of the altar are several objects placed in an orderly sequence. None of which Jovar can identify with any certainty. It seems as though they are probably in the same positions they were in before this great building was vacated. How strange it seemed to Jovar that this appeared to be true.

Why wouldn't the original inhabitants take whatever they could with them if they were planning to leave this place? It is obviously well built with extreme attention to detail. What could have happened to cause such a sudden abandonment? If they had been overcome by an enemy, surely the artifacts would have either been taken or destroyed. Victors accumulate standard trophies of triumph and power, a bloody scrapbook, reminding the kingdoms of their prowess. Returning to the roof, Jovar decides to work on the western roof until evening and then continue the effort the following morning.

As Jovar stirs awake to continue the quest for answers for this new day, his mind recalls the years spent in service to Buovonta. Dedication to duty, excellence, and fulfilling the mission at hand was ingrained in every *sodis* and ackbisk during his days in the kingdom. Despite the context having dramatically changed, it does not alter his resolve to keep unraveling this startling enigma and decide on a strategy once he has concluded to the best of his ability the meanings of the silent testament speaking before him.

As he greets Dohar and prepares for another day by eating the identical food for every meal, his thoughts return to Ilistra, Zalin, and the life that was. Every night he dreams of the reunion, of once again embracing his wonderful family and spending hours in the arms of their love and sharing together the joy that flows and intermingles from the streams of happiness within their spirits.

Is it really possible that he will be successful and return with the ligith branch? Will he ever see them again? Are they doing well without him? Are they able to keep the home in order, both physically and emotionally? Can Zalin keep herself and their daughter calm in the midst of this chaos? His heart begins to feel the agony of even the thought of failing them, and he quickly clenches the deep resolve to return to the assignment that fate has placed on him.

Returning to the roof, Jovar continues cutting away the vines and branches, methodically clearing away the natural coverings, becoming more proficient with each passing hour, knowing the time is approaching to enter into the building itself. Not wanting to injure himself, which would be catastrophic under these circumstances, and not certain if there are any snakes or spiders or other potential adversaries within, the light must be adequate to see exactly what resides in every corner.

There is the option to fashion a torch from the dead vegetation around him rather than bog searching for labyrinth tar and start the fire with his *spignock* stones. But not certain where he is in reference to Sorek, he doesn't want to give any external hint of his presence. However, if the light is not sufficient to adequately identify the contents of the building, a makeshift torch will be used to illuminate the interior. *"Internal victory is the greatest conquest in any warfare."*

REENGAGING THE ENEMY

Battle gear is checked and rechecked before leaving the safety of Sorek. To the surprise of no one, Preven Coluquo has been chosen to lead the expeditionary force to attack Eztrobel. Although it has been over a year since last engaging the kingdom with any significant force, it is felt that a preemptive strike will keep their armies on the defensive rather than giving them any impression of weakness emanating from their own bastion.

The previous conflict produced many casualties for both sides, with most inflicted on Sorek by being outflanked miles before entering their domain. This time there will be many sent out to reconnoiter the perimeters for six miles in each direction to guard against a repeat of the disaster that befell them. They will be sent out in groups of seven, each equipped with a *senfron* to sound an alarm immediately if encountering a large enemy force. Although this may result in casualties or capture, the welfare of the vast majority must be placed above any individual sacrifices that may result.

With twelve hundred warriors strong, the march begins in earnest. There are three main columns that depart in one-hour intervals to avoid congestion and to simultaneously engage any hostilities on several fronts. Knowing that the commanders of Eztrobel are fond of ambushes, the segmenting of forces enables each to come to the other's aid within a reasonable amount of time and keeps their counterparts from outflanking their forces again without placing their own men at risk of being outmaneuvered.

"It seems the weather is cooperating with us, don't you think, Bovelt?" inquires Preven Coluquo.

"Yes, it does, sir," comes the acknowledgment.

The weather cycles tend to vary predictably in seven- to eight-day intervals, depending upon what time of the year it is. Midsummer brings sunshine for about four days, followed by three days of overcast, largely dictated by the patterns created by the Wild Sea. By leaving on the first day of sunshine, the forces will hopefully arrive on the outskirts of Eztrobel on the first overcast evening, which will be ideal circumstances for a concentrated attack.

To move such a large force undetected is quite difficult to achieve. Therefore, an advanced force of five hundred was sent out five days previously to give them time to approach from the south, which will cause Eztrobel to amass a large force to confront them, leaving them more vulnerable to assault from the west. The southern forces are to feign defeat by slowly retreating, drawing Eztrobel's forces farther away from Sorek's main attack body, which will be able to attack with much less resistance. Once the attack commences on the fortress, fires will alert the balance of the southern forces to strike back with unabated energy.

Coluquo feels confident that if their forces can penetrate Eztrobel's defenses and breach a section of the wall in two places, the vulnerability of their kingdom might cause them to surrender or be annihilated within several weeks. If unrelenting pressure is applied to their weakest points, it could cause a rupture of confidence and undermine resilience. Prince Imixam has instructed him to offer life for surrender if the situation turns desperate for the beleaguered enemy.

To have one less kingdom as an adversary would be a great symbiotic victory. Being able to grant a former enemy some measure of internal freedom to make it worth their surrender would spare many lives and reduce the net adversaries to seven. There would obviously have to be a large military presence to ensure the peace, but once disarming the residents of Eztrobel, it would seem that mutual cooperation could proceed. To allow a conquered people to have self-respect and not rape the land, it's people, or it's valuables, gives a great incentive to those triumphed over to remain peaceful.

Although Prince Yexilpar is known for his exceptional prowess in battle, it is thought that he is also a pragmatist when it comes to eradication. It would seem improbable that he would be willing to sacrifice his entire kingdom in a battle that couldn't be won if he could help save the lives of countless of his countrymen. However, the battle has yet to be fought, so it may be premature to already conclude its outcome.

COMMON SOIL

On the third morning, Zalin and Ilistra join their respective mother in the vegetable garden to help with the weeding. The solbon has brought its wonderful warmth, and the lack of clouds portend a pleasant afternoon and evening.

Within a few minutes, Ilistra tires of this extraction exercise and pleads for release. Zalin knows that she has to begin to speak with her mother about the intractable predicament Jovar has inherited, so she suggests her daughter play in the open area beyond them. She can visually keep guard over her as well as being assured of Ilistra's inability to hear the conversation.

After Ilistra's happy departure, Nesigil begins the dialogue. "I know there's trouble, Zalin. Can you tell me about it?"

He mother could be very direct when necessity dictated despite her propensity to circuitous travel paths on almost all inquisitive journeys. A mother knows how to interpret hearts.

Zalin, aware that her mother prefers dispassionate and chronologically orientated explanations, begins by recounting Jovar's miserable declaration that fate-filled day.

After the brief summation, Zalin confesses, "It seems worse than if he had died in battle. I thought I knew what you had gone through, Mother, but now I know I had no idea how awful it has been for you these many years."

Fate has transported them into the same dismal valley of unfathomable grief. There is no substitute for experience.

"Yes," Nesigil responds, "it was hard, and it's still difficult not knowing for certain. My mind has pronounced him dead many times over, but my heart won't acknowledge it. Unless it is somehow proven, I am still hoping he will someday return to us, despite being reminded often how irrational it really is."

As they reflexively embrace each other for a few moments, establishing a freshly forged bond, the tears flow steadily from both sets of eyes, yet with mutual discipline not to appear doing so. Neither do they make any sounds of grief that would alert Ilistra that something awful had transpired. Even though the truth has to be revealed at some point, there is no need to accelerate that revelation, either by accident or casual circumstance.

After returning to the project at hand, two more hours of necessary labor expire until all three are reminded that it is past lunchtime. The cycle of love resumes as though no tears were shed nor hearts pierced. Ilistra will have her portion of unexpected anguish to contend with just like her moms, but now is the season to drink in the pleasures of unfettered living and the unfolding of a mostly perfect world, sprinkled daily with cascades of love and torrents of affection.

REVISITING HISTORY

Dohar's pace instinctively quickens as the long-absent duo nears the entrance into what was the heart of his friend's being. The landscape strangely appears disjointed at first, not what he had been anticipating. The noticeable deterioration of a few of the structures was somewhat understandable, given the length of his absence. But the uneasiness is multiplied by the absence of activity and sound. No Salib. No Ilistra playing outside. No sign of Zalin. Only the erratic hum of nature surrounding him.

Perhaps they had just gone for a visit somewhere for some necessity. Trying not to panic, Jovar quickly dismounts and hastily marches toward the front door. Entering through the same portal he had been escorted out of so many sorrows ago, his fears are vividly realized. There was obviously a struggle or invasion of some sort. But it is just as evident that the disarrayed sight was created months, if not years, ago. All of the hope, the resolve, the intense expectancy are mercilessly crushed in an instant under the cruel finger of fate. Suddenly his whole being groans in anguish, and dreadful reverberations of grief come pouring out of his being, a guttural sigh more than a cry.

"Ahhh—nooo…nooo!" The unabated sorrow profusely and quickly begins to overwhelm his wounded soul.

Suddenly sensing a warm, humid force on his face, his head jerks reflexively away. Temporarily disoriented, he quickly realizes it is Dohar bending over him with a quizzical look in her eyes. Thankfully, there is no homecoming catastrophe. He is still lying down where he had fallen asleep hours ago and still on this side of his quest.

Jovar dreams about his wife and daughter practically every night. But at times, the scenarios are appalling. Making a point of imagining pleasant musings about them before sleep is successful the majority of the time, but occasionally a nightmare makes its wretched presence felt.

Nearing daybreak and unable to rest in peace, Jovar prepares to disrobe the remaining vines from the long clinch of their incidental embrace. The end is clearly within reach. Today should begin the cautious inquisition of the inner sanctum. Only about fifteen lineal feet of vine remains to be severed, which ought to consume seven hours or so.

The *byzevs* are quickly losing their brightness to the eastern horizon. A clear afternoon should provide enough light to venture into the mysterious cavern's western segment. Rediscovering ancient truths necessarily includes a supplementary discovery of one's self. No one can separate completely from the paths traveled by humanity long before personal footprints leave their distinctive marks. *"The past is a preview of the future."*

As the last vine drops to the ground, Jovar has to restrain himself from running on the roof. Intellectually ruminating for the past weeks has only increased the desire for entering the forgotten repository. Although there is light coming from the far western quadrant of the building, it is quickly being extinguished by the steady pace of the approaching evening.

As he anxiously walks to the entryway, he allows his eyes to adjust to the scene dimly illuminated before him. The filtered beams are falling on what appears to be a statue of some sort, several yards below the windows. It gives the impression of having a human form, covered with a long, flowing garment on its head. As Jovar's eyes adjust to the scene, he begins to discern additional similar figures. Long rows of these shapes emerge, each under a corresponding window, all facing inward, toward the altar.

There is not enough light to make out just who or what these represent, but he has seen enough to know it is a solemn place, a location of significance for those who once built and offered obeisance to whatever these silent sentinels represented. Not wanting to get careless and rush in, Jovar lingers a few more moments and retreats to Dohar.

"Well, girl, this has been quite a day for us. Tomorrow we'll get a look at our past and perhaps get an idea of what kind of a society we were once part of. But for now, we both can use some food and water."

Jovar retreats to the well to bring the life-giving liquid to his companion and retrieves some of the occinal fruit to share as well. Although exhausted from the protracted sprint to his initial goal, he will spend the night thinking about the ambiguity that he has just witnessed. It seems logical that at least one of those standing inside would have an Umsnil inscription of some sort on it, given the entry has this feature. He can then pursue the enigma with at least a small measure of veracity, despite the ignorance that currently swallows up the structure. *"Truth often surprises, but never lies."*

Despite the exhaustion, Jovar knows there will be precious little sleep for this fateful evening, as he is seldom able to relax in the midst of impending events, except in battle. Perhaps the example of calm exhibited by his father was the reason for this anomaly. Although there were sparse occasions to witness his father's response to adversity, he couldn't recall any event that caused his father to panic or lose his composure. A perfect consor with absolute resolve, trained to react flawlessly to any circumstance, emotionless as possible—whoever taught him certainly must have been pleased with the results.

For a brief moment, Jovar suddenly wonders if his father is still alive. Or his mother. The emotional distance between his family was immeasurable. He almost never thought about any of them, only on occasions similar to this. It was really a matter of ambivalence. He certainly didn't hate any of them; as a matter of fact, he liked them for the most part. But love was the road not traveled during his tenure with them. He supposes that if they were ever to meet again, he would enjoy it. But the assumption has been that the event will not occur. *"Love withers without nourishment."*

HIDDEN FOR ME

Light is quickly slipping behind the horizon as Zalin and Ilistra walk briskly from the adventure of the day, a visit to the secret pond of Zalin's childhood. Here dreams were dreamed, and laughter bubbled up sweetly from within a soul unaccustomed to grief, sorrow, or anguish. This site of incorruptible days was later replaced with deep longing for a father that did not return home. Zalin only reminisced with Ilistra about the former joys, hoping to infuse her daughter with the same wonder and appreciation for special, hidden enclaves. There are places that need to be preserved for envisioning for those fortunate enough to live in innocent pleasure for a season. The pond would be revisited for the latter soon enough.

"Mommy, wasn't it wonderful to follow the stream up the long hill?"

"Yes, dear, it was something I did every time I came to Hidden for Me."

"Hidden for Me" is the anointed name Zalin declared for this lovely niche of her childhood when she was four years old.

"Sometimes I like it better here than home, because there is so much to explore," Ilistra volunteers. The varying landscape does, in fact, lend itself to the explorer, having many crannies of interest scattered about the generous land. "Although I think I would miss the special places I have back there. You know, Mom, I have a secret place of my own."

Zalin smiles broadly, knowing that this part of growing needs to have that secluded element. "That's good, dear. I'm happy you have that. You don't have to tell me about it, unless you want to share it with me someday when you get older like me. Every little girl needs a secret place, just for her."

The aroma of fresh bread greets the duo before they enter the house. A meal is already waiting with the various smells, intermingling with an inviting combination of welcoming one home.

"Did you have a good time?"

"Yes, Bimmy—the name of endearment Ilistra bestowed on her grandmother when she was two years old—a really fun day of exploring and watching the *feklors* play and jump around in the trees."

"That's so good, isn't it, Ilistra? There is so much to enjoy in this world, isn't there?"

Without any delay, the assorted-aged ladies surround the compact table to enjoy the delights awaiting them.

෬෩෯

The next morning's light breeze slightly cools Zalin's neck and cheeks, her generous, deep-brown hair providing a warmer shelter for the rest of her head. As she quietly sips the hot brew on the front-porch steps, being very careful to first test the rim in the event it's too hot, Jovar again fills her thoughts. *"Ignorance can be an unpleasant companion."* It had been over three months, and she briefly entertains unthinkable thoughts of never seeing his generous smile; his lanky, flexible frame; and the black, compact hair bouncing lightly when he ran.

If her husband wasn't such a loving, self-confident mate and most often correct about his perceptions and predictions, she would have to frankly admit to herself of having no hope at all. It was almost too much to anticipate. To return to her and Ilistra when the vast majority preceding him had simply vanished was too remote a possibility to dwell on for more than a few moments. The empty chamber of her heart was an occasional reminder that *"hope not realized suppresses the soul."*

Quickly realigning her focus, Zalin begins to mentally prepare for the second trip back to the village to meet with her new friends. While determining whether to put on one of her best outfits to appear something she wasn't yet not don garments too dismal to mirror the same, a distant voice reminds her, *One's self is the sum of all the parts.* Another of Wisgraf's much-loved verbal threads also sews into the wardrobe impasse. *Pretense and pretext are both foreign currencies.* Choosing one of her preferred everyday dresses became effortless.

Zalin is beginning to appreciate and anticipate the new cadre of accidental friends that has become a part of her sphere. Still quite cautious about content, she nonetheless feels more relaxed and happy around them. She senses that it is a reciprocal fellowship. After all, each is well aware of the common threads that bind them to one another and practically every other women in the realm.

Once reaching her destination, Zalin effortlessly wades into the multiverbal atmosphere. The discourse traverses the familiar, well-trodden terrain of family and mundane, occasionally meandering into the forests of dreams. The ability to escape the encapsulating sphere of what is and to walk in the realm of what could be is a necessary component of brightening unknown horizons, no matter how irrational some may appear to be. After an elongated and pleasant visit in the forging furnace of mutual interests, the assembled disassemble and retreat to their respective habitats to resume their independent roles incumbent to them.

INCREDIBLE FIGURINES

The morning brings a bright, cloudless sky, perfect for the initial entry for Jovar to begin this venture into history lost. Armed with anticipation, Jovar cautiously steps into the animated book of sculptured interpretations, first looking intently for any kind of movement on the ornate floor. Although mostly covered in dust and various segments of deceased and withered vegetation, there is obviously a pattern of various bright colors of inlaid stone, which appears to include the entire floor area. It may be some type of symbolic representation of the kingdoms, similar to the Sanctor at Kilrek. There is time to uncover that mystery later.

Approaching the carving closest to him, he stands directly in front of it. The most obvious similarity is each figure is bathed in brilliant colors of a type of paint or other material. Muted by the veils of settled dust, it only shades the vividness lying underneath. Showing deference to the object and those that created and venerated it, he refrains from directly touching any part of the creation.

He firmly blows his humid breath onto its facial surface and disrobes the settled dust. It creates an explosion of luminescence. The flowing robe is a liquid light red. As he gazes into the deep-green eyes and gentle face, he confirms that it is a woman, standing resolutely, about a foot above his tall frame. Her graceful hands lightly grasp a vessel, which she appears to be offering to someone or something. There is a wisp of a smile across her lips, which is pleasant to behold.

Her petite feet are wrapped with sandals, with a design unfamiliar to him. An inscription was written upon her pedestal, which was unidentifiable to him. It appeared to be a single word, but he couldn't confirm that at the moment. *"Scorned knowledge is a self-inflicted wound."* As he flashes back to his language classes, of which his interest was less than the chair he was sitting on, he suddenly regrets his self-imposed ignorance. Learning peripherally only for the moment has suddenly exacted its true cost.

His steps etch footprints not formed for countless ages. Although he was not prepared for destiny's abrupt twist of her wrist, it was yet an uncommon privilege to walk in this sacred place as her neophyte guest. He feels strangely honored to enter a realm once revered by countless devotees in communion with one another and to view these replicas now quoting silent creeds. Methodically tracing the sentinels one by one, he slowly traverses the rectangular route. Each sentry is equally elegant and either holding or standing by a symbolic object.

The fifth carving is that of a dark-skinned woman, adorned with a brilliant orange sash, crossing from the back and wrapping around her slender waist. The balance of the outfit is a pleated medium brown, which accents her strikingly serene face. Her hair is pitch black and compact. She is barefoot. By her right side lays a large creature with a pronounced mane surrounding his head that looks simultaneously fierce and confident. Not familiar with the beast, he isn't sure whether it is purely symbolic or representative of some trait, such as courage or great power.

The thirteenth figurine is a deep-brown-eyed young man with a complementary complexion clothed in a light-green robe reaching to his feet. His sinewy arms cradle a large, elaborately decorated scroll. Across the scroll is a word he recognizes. Although the lettering is clearly ancient, it is written in Umsnil.

"Knowledge."

He quickly surmises that the statues probably represent character qualities that people are to exhibit, no matter their origin. If this theory is true, it is clearly not the present state of the kingdoms, including his own.

Actually the reverse is more accurate. What could have caused such a degrading of cultures that the contrary is now the accepted norm? And what about the other unknown kingdoms written on the archway and represented by these effigies? Do they still exist, and if so, where? Clearly this place epitomizes what should be, not what unfortunately is.

A deep feeling of guilt unexpectedly saturates his very soul and covers him with a shroud of death. How many people has he killed in the past eight years? Hundreds to be sure. Was it really necessary? All of the men had families. They left behind wives and children, parents, grandparents, and friends. Being a faithful consor was a great accomplishment, but now he doubts the honor bestowed and the beliefs he has held for his entire life. Was it an absolutely necessary course they had to follow to survive?

Suddenly Wisgraf interrupts his thoughts, *Not everyone who is killed dies.* Strange thought. It is one that he didn't understand the first time he heard it, and he is not sure if he understood now. He knew intellectually that he had to slay those trying to take his life, but now it is certain that there once was a better way to exist for the very kingdoms now engaged in deadly combat and mutual skepticism.

As a deep sigh escapes his lips, he knows intuitively he needs to retreat for a while to compose himself and reflect on these external and internal experiences. Slowly retracing his steps, he exits into the bright day, an exact disparate image of what he has just experienced. As he contemplates the irony, the very optimistic part of his being inserts the illumination that this could also be a sign of what could be again. Immediately, he feels a shedding of the shroud—the prospect that destiny's hand had revisited what could transform the future into a place of safety, peace, and, above all, an environment where love dominates. Perhaps he, Zalin, and Ilistra are signs of what is to come. The thought instantly warms his spirit.

MIZAR ELITE

"Are the men ready to depart?" Coluquo Ulwinc queries.

"Yes, sir. They have been ready for several hours, sir."

"Send them out immediately."

"Yes, sir. Immediately, sir."

As the handpicked eligex depart, their assignment is crucial to the safety of Mizar. Word has reached Sorek that preparations are under way for the kingdoms to unite against them. Sources within Buovonta have been very reliable over the years, so it must be taken seriously.

This reconnaissance team is composed of the premier fighters, interpreters, and interrogators in all of Mizar, perhaps in all the kingdoms combined. Chosen by age five by seasoned eligex from throughout the kingdom, they receive the most complete and intense instruction possible. Tempered over the years not to manifest any weaknesses of body, spirit, or mind, they are without question an unparalleled force. Not having a wife or family of any sort, their commitment is to Mizar alone.

There has never been an eligex betrayer in the history of the kingdom. None has ever been captured. Total devotion is their life's blood. They never fail to complete their assignment. The contingent relishes yet another occasion to execute their skills for the sake of their beloved kingdom. *"Loyalty grafted with excellence produces the fruit of victory."* The privilege is theirs; the consequences belong to those who resist them.

⟨⟩⁕⟨⟩

Deciding to wait another day before ruminating on additional revelations that lie in wait for him, Jovar decides to take Dohar for a ride around the previous perimeter and perhaps explore a wider diameter and see what lies beyond his immediate horizon. Never content just to see only what lies in front of him, his heart yearns to seek horizons yet discovered. He has plenty of speculating to carry out during the brief expedition. Or perhaps nature will instead provide a succinct season of relief to an already-overworked voyager.

As he mounts Dohar, unforeseen satisfaction floods Jovar. To return, however briefly, to the commonplace blunts the uncertainty regularly assaulting his mind. *"Walking in resolve is the path that leads to success,"* those words abruptly breathe literal energy into his spirit.

Lightly touching the flanks, in whispered tones, he asks his friend, "Well, girl, it's good to move out again, isn't it?"

The two companions have a dialogue that the other understands very well. *"Communication is great treasure to those who discern its worth."* The duo leisurely head slightly northwest, to nowhere in particular, to explore and restore. Truly feeling relaxed for perhaps the first time since the darkness pervaded his family, he feels confidence arising to challenge the persistent pockets of internal warfare.

As their collective excursion reaches about fifteen minutes through the dense vegetation, Jovar decides to retrace his steps, having drawn a precise mental map of the course he has inscribed, knowing the importance of returning to his temporary and enlightening refuge. During this brief hiatus, his thoughts have predictably varied between Zalin and Ilistra and the new discovery.

Without warning, Dohar suddenly snorts, drops quickly to her knees, and rapidly lies down on her left side. Although initially startled, Jovar knows there is only one reason he is now lying on the ground next to Dohar. He will certainly be captured within moments. *"A crisis demands creativity."*

After several tense moments, he hears the sound of several feet running quickly toward his position. A strong voice commands in Pefghal, "Get up."

As he obediently arises, he immediately recognizes his captors as members of the Bitter Scourge, a name his fellow officers dubbed this particular element of Fortress Sorek. Although anticipating to be killed within moments, he quickly decides not to reach for the easily identified sword on his right hip, for doing so would mean certain death.

A well-hewn and conditioned eligex approaches and stands within a breath's length from Jovar's face, peering intently into his eyes. He knows the officer will begin asking questions and will be expecting answers.

"What is your name, consor?"

"Jovar, sir."

"What are you doing out here?"

"I was banished from the kingdom."

"Why were you banished from Buovonta?"

"Some of my men were killed by your men."

"I see. Remove his sword and take charge of him, Besulgan."

"Yes, sir."

Genuinely surprised to be still alive, Jovar is somewhat relieved, at least for the moment, to be captured rather than dispatched. *"Time becomes invaluable when very little remains."*

He and Dohar are immediately escorted in the same direction they were heading on their own, but now by a band of six well-armed warriors, supposedly to Sorek.

He assumes if they had wanted to kill him, they would have already done so. Told to look straight ahead, he dares to not visually wander, but his ears perceive a large force heading south, not far west from where they were venturing, apparently heading to Fortress Kilrek.

CONSTRUCTING THE SNARE

Madnak convenes the assembled in the Sanctor, the leaders forming a generously spaced kaleidoscope semicircle around the imposing mosaic. Well-armed guards place themselves directly behind their respective seated commanders.

Madnak slowly rises and positions himself squarely upon the facsimile of Sorek and stares silently at their universal antagonist.

After a few moments, he begins to speak, methodically shifting to peer into each participant's eyes, "Friends of freedom, I thank you for accepting the invitation to come to Buovonta. Although we are very diverse in appearance, we share the same desire to destroy our common enemy. We have allowed our differences to divide us, instead of building upon our shared foundation. We have permitted our customs, our dress, our appearance, and our forms of leadership to separate us. We must overcome our own intolerance of one another or continue to be overcome by the Mizar. I would ask you to look at one another for a few moments, realizing we all share the same goal concerning Fortress Sorek."

Unaccustomed to taking orders, after a lengthy pause, each begins to inspect the other, keeping their opinions to themselves, masking their emotions, not revealing any hint of what was in their minds.

After a few moments, Madnak continues, "As we look at one another, we see dark skin, such as we share with the kingdom of Drevkrez and the Mizar. Others of you are light skinned in appearance, and a few have hues in between. Our weapons also vary, but each has their value against the enemy. I would ask that we begin to share our thoughts of how to finally defeat Sorek, by using our collective strengths to destroy them. As I mentioned in the invitation, I requested that each one come prepared to offer a suggestion on how to accomplish our goal. Why don't we begin with Prince Yexilpar of Eztrobel on my left and continue in order around our circle? And if you would please continue to speak in Pefghal so no one will need an interpreter."

As Prince Madnak expected, each leader expressed the superiority of their form of combat to defeat Sorek, some quite animated, others with a matter-of-fact demeanor. One by one, they reminded the others of the efficacy of their approach.

When the final presentation was concluded, Prince Madnak spoke again, "My friends, I am impressed with all of your suggestions. Your singular strengths and unique assets are without question formidable and would prove insurmountable against the Mizars if used cooperatively. I do believe we will be using our particular skills and techniques together against Sorek. It is not a question of whether we will but when and how. What I'm about to propose will likely initially sound to you as ridiculous or insane, but I would request you hear me out until I fully explain my plan."

Madnak begins to spin his web as well as any seasoned spider. Strand by strand, he methodically weaves a pattern deeper into their reservations until he perceives a communal resolve beginning to adhere to his silk embroidery. The integrated and enumerated theme of deceiving their historical rival visibly appealed to several of the gathered, as numerous leaders manifested a slight grin or smirk as the plan was unfolded.

After several minutes, Madnak ends the monologue and asks for comments.

The first to speak was Imixam, prince of Tyvrens. "I must say that you were right. It did sound insane, but I think your plan has some merit, especially because we have never been able to overcome their fortress by ourselves. Pretending to acquiesce is quite frankly brilliant, in my option. However, I see difficulty in keeping up the charade for a lengthy period of time. Several years seem to be too long of a time to wait to strike."

To no one's surprise, Brivel, prince of Fruwmunjie, suddenly erupts, demanding that all concerned immediately prepare to attack Sorek and fight to the last person, whether it be them or the Mizars. Their reputation for irate, irrational, and unpredictable behavior is confirmed yet again.

No one interjects to voice disagreement, which would guarantee a verbal, if not physical, melee. The atmosphere is permitted a respectable interval to subside before another voice offers comment.

The balance of the input is tepid, not endorsing but neither rejecting Madnak's vision. It is clear to Madnak that the initial meeting has met his expectations. Several more interchanges should solidify his overall plan. The entourage is presently recessed to the banquet hall to enjoy specialties from each kingdom, adding planks to the bridge of communion between them that will hopefully tolerate the stress of united warfare.

UNIMAGINED EXPECTATIONS

As the harvest of the *zilvah* approaches, Zalin and Ilistra are busy preparing for the work ahead. Now several inches taller, Ilistra has long since stopped asking about her father, knowing intuitively that she will never see him again. The forced absence has changed both her and her mother in the two years since his mysterious departure. Remaining at her grandmother's has been helpful, removed from the familiar setting of what once was, not having to be reminded daily of something that can never be recaptured.

Zalin has outwardly adapted to the new reality as well, however, not giving up hope in her resourceful husband. Believing him to be dead would be her own death. Ilistra needs her to be a strong example of inner strength, despite the internal grief that never departs her spirit concerning Jovar. *"Half of something is better than all of nothing."*

The initial trip back to their home was also their last. Their home and contents were turned over to another consor's family within three months of Jovar's exile. To be greeted by strangers at the door of your own home was shocking to be sure, but just one more reason to reject the mind-set of this kingdom. What family she had left in her hands was to be grasped with resolve.

Zalin has yet to confide with any depth about the real circumstances surrounding her emotionally tattered threadbare existence with her casual acquaintances. The charade must continue without deviation to ensure absolute security for her family and their future. Not being able to trust those around her causes an inner conflict, but resolve is an abundant commodity within her soul.

Although Ilistra has appeared to adjusted to her absent father, Zalin doesn't think her daughter believes the worst. The promise of tomorrow, however vague and unrealistic it may seem at times, still eclipses the ever-encroaching despair, lurking in the shadows of her life, waiting to overcome her if she dares to cease believing.

What she does not know is at that very moment, Jovar is sitting down on the edge of the field assigned to him to eat the doled-out rations with his *qalsh*. He happens to sit near one of the *cenkkors*, who is addressing those under his charge from an adjacent group.

An overheard phrase jolts him to commands he really has no interest in overhearing. "Be quick about it. Time has no time for you."

The only other person whom he ever heard speak those words was Zalin, and always in a light-hearted manner.

He instantly rises toward the speaker. Although he is not authorized to speak with a cenkkor from another qalsh, he knows he must approach this older man. Thankfully, he is only yards away, and the guards probably won't notice his trespass.

"Excuse me, sir, but may I ask you a question?"

The old man turns and faces the inquirer without emotion. "Yes, you may." He too undoubtedly knows the law, but appears unafraid.

"I have only heard that phrase from one other person in the world. Her name is Zalin. Do you happen to know her?"

The blood instantly leaves the man's face, and the stranger almost collapses.

Jovar reflexively grabs his arm so he doesn't crumple. He is now certain he has just met Zalin's father, or at least a close relative. "Are you Hilophil?"

"Yes, I am."

"Well, I am Jovar, Zalin's husband."

Both father-in-law and son-in-law stare in bewilderment, unable to fully absorb such an incredible revelation.

Hilophil quickly and tersely retorts, "We will speak again."

Without further delay, Hilophil abruptly turns toward his charges and reenters the assigned patch of fresh produce. There will be little sleep tonight for each recipient powerfully swayed by the emotional tremor they had just experienced.

Still reeling from the brief encounter, Jovar can only imagine the absolute joy Zalin would have in knowing that her father lives. A resurrection from the dead is not an everyday occurrence. However, the fields of Sorek are a great distance from the arms of his wife, daughter, and son. Impossible, it would seem. But then the impossible just materialized in front of his eyes.

A tender plant began to sprout another leaf in Jovar's garden of hope for his own reunion. Perhaps he and Hilophil would have another opportunity to meet and begin planning a long-term solution. Perhaps he could find a way to be transferred into his father-in-law's qalsh.

This development would have to undergo detailed analysis and contingency considerations. The ultimate goal would be to escape and to return home. However, that possibility will take much covert investigation. Undoubtedly, there are scores of individuals like themselves who long to return as well. However, there are certainly spies among the qalshes, and one mistake would lead to permanent loss. If one is discovered to be involved in an escape plan, the penalty is public execution. There are also rewards given to those who point out the plotters. If they are successful, they will never return, if not they will be put to death. One thing is certain—*"one must outwit the wise without revealing their ignorance."*

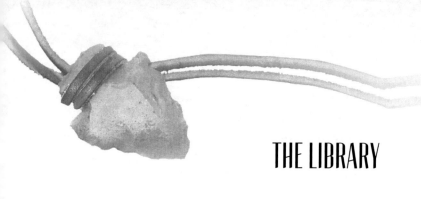

THE LIBRARY

As the final preparations for the imminent betrayal are coordinated by the various commanders assembled at Kilrek, Madnak impulsively decides to venture into the library of princes. Not one for excessive reading, let alone studying, he calls for an interpreter to recite from the histories of past leaders to compare their judgments to his own. He is confident his strategy will be viewed for millennia as the mark of genius. The prince has had a recorder of his own choices since he assumed the responsibility to lead. The public version of events is written in the language of the kingdom for use in the learning centers.

However, the library of princes was another realm, not accessible to any but the current prince. The clandestine repository contained private texts and were written in ancient Leginus, a long since–forgotten and written language of some past culture. The reason was to keep certain accounts secret from the rest of the kingdom for security purposes.

The group of interpreters were given a wide berth of privileges and were allowed to have families in a segregated section of the kingdom, which was unknown to the population as a whole. Not even the sodii who guarded and protected them knew the true reason for their existence. Any breach of security from either guard or the guarded was an immediate death sentence.

Madnak instructs the reader to begin with the most recent ruler preceding him, Prince Hyzelion. Also from a similar background to his, Prince Madnak absorbs the information about the tactics of his predecessor, agreeing in spirit with the majority of his decisions.

Suddenly he is staggered as the interpreter recounts an event that occurred in the kingdom when he was a child. Prince Hyzelion had ordered his own personal elite troops to secretly kill whole families within the kingdom from time to time and to make certain it was blamed on the Mizars. One such place was Selisom, his place of birth. He was told that his parents and siblings were slain by the Mizar while he was away visiting his cousins for two weeks. Ever since that awful event, he had despised the Mizar and made it his life's goal to avenge their deaths. He suddenly realizes everything he was told about them was a lie.

The revelation nearly causes Madnak to vomit. He immediately halts the reading and instructs the reader to exit. Left alone to reflect on this horrible epiphany, he cannot fully grasp what he has just heard. It is inconceivable that a prince of Buovonta would knowingly and willingly shed innocent blood of his own heritage, regardless of the perceived benefit. However, now he knows his own family's blood was shed for political reasons. Who knows how many more lies have been told over the centuries in the name of freedom?

Powerful emotions wash over Madnak as he reflects on the significance of what this personally means to

him and his plans to destroy Sorek. It will take time to absorb and evaluate this drastic disclosure, a commodity of which he has very little of left.

But he is suddenly certain of one thing—he cannot participate with the plan he so eagerly birthed and nurtured for so long. To do so would violate and destroy his own internal spirit and render him shattered for the balance of his life. *"If one does not possess integrity, he is the most impoverished of all."* Unsure of the consequences ahead, he is compelled by only what not to do.

⌒⦶⦶⌒

The tone of the meeting hall is clearly anticipatory and reminded Madnak of some of the early years before he became a prince. The zeal of attacking the enemy and the certainty of victory, whether real or imagined, filled the emotional nostrils of the assembled. The long delay was over. The phony overtures of friendship and prisoner exchanges were cautiously received. The additional admission of leaders into the other's realms, although limited, was also carried out successfully with the cloak of deception fully covering the real intent of the faux peacemakers.

"My friends, I need to tell you something now that you will probably not believe, but I must inform you of recent revelations that have completely altered my thinking."

Madnak begins by recounting the hatred that formed as a child for the Mizars at the death of his parents and siblings and the incessant plotting and consuming passion that enveloped his life from that point on. Then without revealing the source of his information, he reports that he has absolute proof that the Mizar were not responsible for the death of his family as he had been told.

"Therefore, I cannot or will not commit any of our resources to this venture. Furthermore, I plan to send an emissary immediately to the Mizars to try to establish real peace with them on behalf of Buovonta."

The stunned recipients are dazed in disbelief. Without warning, Prince Brivel rushes headlong into Prince Madnak, screaming, "Traitor!" And he plunges a previously concealed knife into Madnak's stomach and violently rips it upward.

The prince lurches backward and falls to the floor without a word, just gasping briefly before becoming motionless.

Brivel, looking crazed, swiftly pivots around the entire assembly, Madnak's blood drenching his hands, his eyes flashing. No one else dares move, knowing that any reaction will result in complete chaos and further carnage. All of the guards also remain at their posts, including those of Buovonta, knowing the certain outcome of further aggression.

"We are going to destroy the Mizars without delay," bellows Brivel. "Madnak was a traitor, and if Buovonta will not join us, so be it, but they must not interfere, or they too will be destroyed without mercy."

Silence dominates the surreal landscape for long, tense moments.

Prince Imixam, known in his kingdom for his wisdom, speaks. "We obviously have had a dramatic change of circumstances. I suggest we take a few

moments to think through in our own minds what just transpired, retreat into our personal enclaves, and reconvene in two hours."

The balance of the leaders look at one another and nod their approval. If nothing else, it will provide some space to evaluate the dramatic, unexpected shift and remove them all from the volatile Brivel and his explosive presence. Without further delay, all slowly rise without speaking and leave the bloody scene.

Prince Brivel remains until all others have exited, still looming over his latest casualty, glaring at the princes as each walks away.

⁕

The combined forces begin their coordinated and altered plans with a renewed sense of resolve. Time is not a friend to any given the recent developments. Alliances tend to be fragile commodities.

The death of Madnak actually works in favor of the more moderate factions. Giving Brivel and his forces the lead in the frontal attack will ensure large casualties on all the participants. The less survivors from both sides, the better. If Brivel and his warriors survive in large numbers, the covert contingency plan will have to be implemented swiftly.

The ackbisk commander, Zeymilve, has agreed to coordinate in Madnak's stead. The official reports say that Madnak unexpectedly attacked Brivel, resulting in his own death. The Kilrek sodii present at the execution of Prince Madnak were also slain, while supposedly participating in the same melee against Brivel and his guards. Given the well-known disposition of both leaders, no one suspects anything is amiss.

It will take several weeks for everyone to assume their positions. Undoubtedly, there will be missteps; however, each prince must keep the primary goal in mind at all times and adapt accordingly. Inadvertent contact with the enemy is practically inevitable, but resolution must occur swiftly and without any enemy survivors to ensure surprise. Once the Cyvehs initiate the attack, the balance of forces will move swiftly to gain their advantage.

The initial assault is not meant to immediately end the kingdom, but strike the initial blow to weaken it. Each of the realms has as a separate assignment on disabling an aspect of the Mizar host, specific to their unique skills. Every aspect of Sorek's survival will be addressed—food, water, land, captives, and resources. It will be victory by decree and degree. The length of the clash may linger for a season, but the flame of Sorek will be surely be extinguished, never to be reignited.

EDGE OF VICTORY

As several weeks pass, the various armed kingdoms have managed to arrive at their predetermined positions without serious incident. Only three of the forces encountered enemy contact, but all three were able to completely decimate the smaller bands with overwhelming force. Of course, there were no prisoners taken.

The Cyveh advance group has arrived at the outer edge of Fortress Sorek itself, observing the massive outline in the evening shadows, protruding as some dark, forbidden gemstone. Before daybreak, the massive assault will commence. Given the fact that there is a seven-mile perimeter surrounding the fortress with virtually no cover, save for the harvest fields, they know they will be discovered quickly.

For the Cyveh, this is ideal. The prospect of combat in an open area, face-to-face with the adversary, delights them. No enemy can match their agility or fierceness. They have a well-earned reputation for brutality and for being absolutely merciless. *"Fear debilitates. Calm facilitates."* The anticipation is profusely stimulating to these fighters and provides them with abundant energy for the task ahead.

As Jovar dutifully gathers yet another unnumbered basket of grain, his thoughts have exponentially expanded to seeing Zalin again. It has become more difficult to concentrate on the task at hand, which is unwise, given the severity of punishment to the lax. Although somewhat humane, they are also brutal taskmasters, not sparing the less-than-enthusiastic slaves, doling out physical pain and, in extreme cases, death. Keeping an obviously hostile force in compliance requires measures not required to the friendly, but essential to those less accommodating. *"Goodness in not always clothed in white."*

As the evening approaches, it beckons both the laborers and the overseers to finish the tasks before them. Within minutes, the shadows of a waning day bring the occasion of reprieve for those charged with the yield. Rest is required for man and creature alike, whether they seem to be identical in the eyes of the destiny withholders or not. Another opportunity to revive the body with a brief interlude is a welcome addition for the captured beasts of burden. None in or over the fields is aware that tomorrow will not remotely resemble the day just ending.

As the preliminary bodies of the forces methodically close toward their prey just before daybreak, they all notice a significant increase in the cloud cover. The wind is also beginning to make its presence known; at first it is just a light breeze, but now it appears to be

gathering momentum. There is also an unexpected and unusual chill beginning to envelop them.

On the plateau of Sorek, these same signs are not going unnoticed. Being much higher in altitude, the swift movement of the clouds is very apparent, and the winds are quickly increasing. The waves of the Wild Sea are also commencing to grow larger. Within a few more minutes, the new light reveals the waves are becoming white and frothing, enlarging and increasing in amplitude and elevation. It is becoming obvious that a major storm is rapidly approaching. Although storms are not uncommon for this sea, its name being representative of its nature, those viewing the briskness and power are sensing that this may become very intense.

The balance of the assault forces have assembled themselves in a large semicircle from the center of the Mizar kingdom. Approximately half of each of the kingdoms' military might are only three hours from the initial strike and will begin their march at daybreak, while the balance of the forces remain two days back, if more force is necessary.

The second phase of the operation is to quickly reinforce the original forces on the ground with an overwhelming number, which will force the Mizar defenders to retreat to their impenetrable plateau, thus voluntarily isolating themselves from any possible further attack, and also ensure that they will have no possible means of escape.

The third part of the plan involves initially constructing scaffolding directly behind the massive trees that face the plateau to avoid any counterattack of the Mizars while the scaffolding is under construction. When completed, platforms will be erected from which to inundate the exalted site with the plagues from Lybukom. Dispensed from improvised catapults, custom-made for the unique surroundings, anchored about a hundred feet in the air, they will hurl certain death on the huddled, encapsulated adversaries.

Naturally building on such a massive scale will take time. However, their enemies wouldn't be going anywhere, and there would be no particular deadline to meet, so it could proceed in an orderly fashion, with no reason to be too hasty or careless. The day would arrive when the projectiles would be unleashed, and then rotted flesh would rot the flesh of the whole Mizar kingdom until all would be dissolved and swallowed by the cold throat of death. Cleanup afterward would simply be burning anything and everything remaining on the elevated plain.

As the bands of Cyveh pressed eagerly ahead, it was becoming apparent to even the most zealous that if the rapidly enhancing tempest continued, it would become impossible to engage the enemy. Already they were feeling the force of the rain, literally stinging them on their exposed skin. Erratically flying sideways and multiplying in velocity, the liquid arrows penetrated the senses and threatened their eyesight.

Within a few more moments, it seemed prudent to halt the advance and take cover in the yet-to-be-harvested fields they were marching alongside. Orders were given. It seemed unlikely anyone had seen them approach at this point because visibility was rapidly deteriorating to near zero. Within an instant after the command, all the Cyvehs melted into the high foliage and literally vanished, awaiting further instruction.

Zalin and her mother had gone to work in their fields at dawn and returned home several hours after first light to eat breakfast and rest for a while. The weather is now cooler and not as taxing as it was in the high summer months.

However, without warning, the wind abruptly increases in intensity and soon becomes very strong and dangerous. This increasingly ferocious gale was garnished with a massive momentum, and the trio began securing everything they could and withdrawing to the lee side of the sturdiest structure they knew of, the sturdy food-storage facility.

Although realizing it might cost them their lives, they hastily determined to attempt to reach the secure cave nestled in the Hidden for Me haven, knowing it would withstand any force that might still be approaching.

The ferocious wind was at their back, which to them seemed to be the additional power they would need to reach their goal. They would soon know the wisdom or folly of this critical decision.

A FISSURE OPPORTUNITY

Within minutes of the unexpected crisis, the guards herded their charges into the vast refuge at the southern base of the fortress. All of the prisoners were ushered into the large fissure that provided safety from this extreme environment. Any additional Mizars who were in the vicinity would also rush toward this haven if possible. Those residents at the top of Sorek had no time to descend, but adequate structures had been erected centuries earlier to provide a sufficient shield for such events.

The rear of the natural habitat housed a large cache of food staples, clothing, weapons, torches, and other miscellaneous items set aside for unforeseen crises, of which this qualified. However, the contents were secured with specialized locks, the keys of which were held by a select few high officials, none of whom were among the gathered. This posed a conundrum for the several low-level Mizar authorities within the confines.

It was very evident to everyone in the predicament, both free and slave, that a thin sliver of escape was presenting itself. The few in charge of the many knew they had inadequate power to restrain their captives if they chose to rebel. Words can restrain the willing, and weapons speak with deadly clarity to all. However, applying lethal force in this circumstance may end their personal existence as well. Outnumbered at least twenty to one are not favorable odds when considering your immediate future in a hostile environment.

Beyond that reality, opening up the reserve by force would necessarily create access of the same to their enemies, which by any measure of logic would be deemed insane. Even though it was a treasonable offense punishable by death for aiding the escape of any prisoner, the unspoken mandate for the guards in this situation was going to be survival, not heroics. In their minds, choosing to end one's life in a useless attempt at restraining the insurmountable was idiotic, not noble, and none had the penchant to play the fool. Although this unwritten impromptu policy would not be uttered, it would be adhered to.

Because the torches were not accessible, only natural light would be available to illumine the plateau's womb. When that subsided, it would be impossible to see very far in any direction. Yet still early in the day, even though the relentless torrents dimmed the sky as an opaque liquid cloak, there was still enough light to clearly discern individuals swirling within this human sea. As Jovar entered the elevated floor of the cavern, along with several hundred other sudden refugees, he immediately began to scan the human horizon for his father-in-law. Moving quickly and methodically, he slips among the immigrant population to find his newly discovered relative. Undoubtedly, Hilophil would be doing the same.

Within the hour, their destinies meet on the shelf not far from their escape route, the right side of the fissure, which has several natural ground features to allow for stealth movement. Although they are surrounded by countless ears, most were too preoccupied with themselves to care what others said. Jovar begins speaking in whispered tones. As Zalin was well aware, Jovar would at times be completely out of character and utter words that one could not anticipate. "We have to act quickly, Hilophel, because time has no time for us."

Hilophel smiles deeply at the wit and optimism of his son-in-law. "Yes," he replies. "It will have to be after nightfall regardless of the conditions."

They both wander closer to the entrance but keep a respectful distance away so as not to alert searching eyes. Although there will be several guards at the entrance throughout the night, it will be virtually impossible to see anyone once night falls on them all.

However, after the initial confusion and disorder had somewhat subsided within this cauldron of chaos, the human chalice of diversity begin to mirror a strange aura of peace completely antithetical to the environs. It may have been ushered in by the great gift of life still possessed by the assembled. Perhaps it was partially birthed by breathing in an irrational atmosphere of freedom, which none of the unblessed had inhaled for some time.

Whatever the causes, a sense of thankfulness begins to pervade the cavern like some irresistible, enveloping fog. It seemed both external and internal peace blossomed in the midst of bedlam. The common bonds of humanity were apparently drinking from the same life-sustaining well of happiness of what is at the moment, rather from the charted waters of what was or the elusive maps of what is to come. *"To be thankful for the breath and breadth of life brings great contentment."*

As the inevitable, inky veil began imposing its will on the premises, the reunited duo assumed they wouldn't be the only ones attempting to slink into the blackness. However, it was not their intent to organize or lead any mass exodus, but rather exit without sound or notice.

Although they had been captured decades apart, their entrance into the Mizars' lair was the same: the labyrinth. Therefore their initial entrance route would also serve as an exit to the anticipated reunion with loves lost. Now realizing that the lore of the emerald consumer of countless lives was probably more propaganda than fact, they could proceed with some measure of speed, yet not summarily dismissing it or the reality that there still remained real enemies surrounding them.

When fully immersed in the tarlike sphere, they methodically crept next to the right wall and stopped every few feet to listen to any sounds in front of them. *"Senses elevate when danger lurks."* Hilophil led the tiny caravan for an hour's minuscule pace without incident to the periphery of their initial destination. They had also correctly surmised that the guards present would most likely not try to kill any of the captives for fear of being killed themselves.

However, as they began to leave the safety of the cavern, a sudden escalation of voices about forty-five feet to their immediate left alerted them to an apparent scuffle taking place. Without delay, they began to walk quickly straight ahead. Because the fierce winds and rain were still blowing from the north, the south side was relatively navigable for about one hundred feet. But once they crossed over that line of demarcation, they were in the unrelenting stream of turmoil. They had planned to walk slowly in as straight a line as possible, having tied themselves together with some of the bundling twine they used to secure the grains in the fields.

Once they reached the relative safety of the tree line, they would try to find some cover and rest until daylight. They anticipated the storm would begin to subside in a day or two, which would put them well away from the fortress. When the Mizars begin the process of ascertaining their losses of crops, property, citizens, and workforce, they will surely thoroughly search the immediate areas first and would not have the time nor resources to look for wayward slaves.

As the gale aided their progress, it also required great energy to stay upright and focused on their goal. After repeatedly falling down and being blown about, they finally reached the tree line while still quite dark. Totally exhausted and suffering from dehydration and cold, they huddled together on the lee side of a giant fir and quickly fell asleep. The first steps of a new life had been trod.

ROCKY REFUGE

Thankfully the secret place was just close enough to reach before it would have been forever beyond their grasp. Fortunately as well, the cave in the secret garden entrance was facing south. It was also elevated, so the three climbed into their rock nest to relative comfort. The entrance was adequately large for Salib to find safety as well. They had taken their faithful companion to use as a shield as well as a source of strength in a desperate symbiotic journey of preservation.

Although they only carried on their persons enough food for several days, there was plenty of drinkable water only yards away. Also knowing that no storm lasts forever, the primary difficulty remaining would likely be the ability to sleep adequately in the impenetrable bedroom. "Comfort is seen through the eyes of circumstance"—another apropos Wisgrafian adage roosts on their literally stony shelf.

The initial conversation revolved around their harrowing passage and modestly congratulating themselves for making a wise decision, which was appropriate given the consequences of making a potentially fatal choice. Yet Zalin's heart was always searching for Jovar, and she wondered aloud if he was still alive and if he would have made it through this latest manifestation of nature's hemorrhaging.

Nesigil, fully aware of thinking the very same thoughts as her daughter when Hilophil had vanished, had no interest is reiterating her reality but tersely replied, "Of course, he would." Zalin quickly thanked her for her reassurance although she assumed her mother was simply speaking to her heart and not her head. Her mother's motives or intent didn't really matter; what did matter was her desire to keep her hope breathing so she could emotionally exhale as well.

Two more days pass before the fury begins to abate. Not wanting to proceed prematurely, they agree to wait until the wind and rain decreased sufficiently to return without fear of injury. There was still more than a day's supply of food, and their adopted refuge was adequate for the moment, so there was no real need to risk their security for time's sake.

By evening, the weather pattern was clearly losing its deadly grip, and the decision to proceed home was agreed upon. The light was still bright enough to light their paths, which also revealed the massive destruction that was apparent all around them. Many trees had been uprooted, but to their surprise, the majority of the fields of grain were still intact, with only certain patches flattened by the fierce winds. Debris from who knows where littered the area as makeshift letters randomly delivered to no one in particular. *"Nature has its own form of delivering messages."*

Within a few hundred feet from their home, to their collective relief, it was plain that it had withstood the onslaught with minimal damage. Hilophil had a reputation for overbuilding anything and everything, and the house stood as a testament to his spirit of

excellence and wisdom. It was also obvious that all of the outbuildings remained firm where Hilophil had planted them. A smile of thanks formed on Nesigil's well-weathered yet delicate face. Her mind instantly returned to the happier days when her husband was constructing their sanctuary and the hectic pace of raising children and regularly going off to fight a relentless foe. Even after these many years, her heart still yearned for the man who went off to war and didn't come back.

As they entered the kitchen area, all stomachs were ready for some substance. Nesigil retrieved some preserves and fresh produce that were stored in the underground cellar, which kept foods in relatively good condition for long periods of time. It was then decided to begin an inventory the next day to access the casualties of the onslaught. It appeared that some of their grain had been badly damaged, and the garden had likely suffered loss as well. However, the barn animals had all survived, and that was counted a victory in the undeclared war.

Within a week, it was apparent that even though a lot of grain had been lost, they had adequate reserves from the previous year, which had been a record harvest, another reason to give thanks for unanticipated favor. Zalin had been very careful to instruct Ilistra of the ways of the farm, and her daughter had been both observant and proactive in all the aspects of her duties—all but cleaning up after the animals. But no one really enjoys that chore, including Zalin. But she alternated with her daughter to share in the unpleasant duty to remind herself and her daughter that *"willing sacrifice is foundational to a life well lived."*

REDISCOVERING FAMILY

As Jovar and Hilophil awoke before dawn, they agreed to press ahead and put as much distance between themselves and the Mizars as quickly as possible. *"Freedom demands blood."* They didn't want it to be theirs. Although Jovar still had all the skills as a warrior that he possessed before his capture, the zeal to attack his enemy had diminished. It wasn't that he agreed with them or that he didn't realize that war was inevitable, but his brief interlude in the temple began to change him internally. However, if he had to kill someone to secure his freedom and that of his family, he would not hesitate.

Hilophil was less gracious. For years, he resented being separated from his faithful wife and raising a family together because of the Mizars. Although he was begrudgingly grateful for not being killed, he felt it was similar to be thankful if someone beats you only two times a day rather than three. "Time has no substitute." Once it has been spent, it is impossible to retrieve it. It was primarily a robbery of his dreams and passions that grated his soul. More than once he had thought of ending his own misery, but each time the spirit within him would not give up on the possibility of somehow attaining freedom. He had dreamed many scenarios over the decades, but never this one. He too was not going to squander the chance if someone tried to prevent him from reuniting with his family. They would die, not him.

Within a few steps of the first whole day of freedom, they began to talk about their respective families. Jovar had told him that his wife was alive and doing well, for which Hilophil was very grateful. Jovar also mentioned that he assumed that Zalin would have ventured to Zwenvestin sometime ago and would probably still be there. Hilophil surmises that they would have survived this storm because he built things to last and knew his wife would either go down to the cellar or to the cave. He assures Jovar that they will see them all again.

Jovar then gave Hilophil an extended description of Ilistra: her characteristics, her appearance, which resembles Zalin's side of the family, and countless other details. Hilophil enjoyed hearing about the granddaughter whom he had never met and didn't know existed. Jovar couldn't comment on Filoquaid as he hadn't seen him since they were married, because he was assigned to a specialized band that is basically sequestered for the length of their duty. Neither he nor Zalin frankly know if he was still alive, although the authorities generally inform the survivors of the death of a sodus.

The discussion then turned toward how they each found themselves in this predicament. Hilophil was part of an advanced party when he was captured by the eligex. Several of his companions foolishly attacked the overwhelming force and were immediately killed. He and twelve others were spared. He occasionally has had opportunities to briefly talk with his former sodii, but only on official topics because their guards are always within earshot.

As Jovar recounts his path to the present, he eventually brings up the temple to Hilophil. As he describes what he saw, Hilophil's demeanor becomes intense. There is no question this information has drawn another heart into the arena of aspiration. Jovar hopes he will wander near the path they took from the temple area so Hilophil can see for himself.

To know that their predecessors had lived a far superior and harmonious existence together was both the illness and the cure. Yes, he knew there didn't seem to be any way to change the nine kingdoms, but the temple proved otherwise. There was a time that they did live in peace and mutual respect, not to mention the other missing kingdoms. What did they possess that the present generations did not? What event or events caused such a drastic departure from harmony to hostility—not only that but also to last for centuries? In his heart, Jovar knew that because it happened in the past, there would be a way to have it resurrected in the future. How? Perhaps it would have to start with himself.

Although both men did not recognize exactly where they were in the labyrinth, they knew if they headed due south, they would eventually come to the edge of Buovonta. From there they would find a means to get home. *"Passion is always the pioneer."*

BATTLE ENGAGED

Although the forces aligned against Sorek had suffered loss and communication had been severed, at least one segment was determined to continue. Brivel and his forces had never retreated from any battle. They had waited too long to allow the weather to thwart their opportunity to rid themselves of an enemy within arrow, knife, or sword's reach.

Just after midnight of the third evening, as the storm began to abate, Brivel had already assembled about two hundred of his forces. He immediately began to lead them in a slow run towards the rock pillar. Their emphasis on being the strongest and fittest fighters in the realm allowed them to quickly cover the distance to their initial objective without becoming exhausted. Well before daylight they were at the foot of the hidden roadway leading to the crest of the fortress. Their source from Kilrek had given them accurate information about the access point. Within a short while it would become apparent if she had been just as accurate about the layout of the fortress itself.

Brivel assumed their adversaries would only be thinking of recovery, not defense. Thirty minutes later they were peering into their enemy's liar. Weeks earlier they had rehearsed their respective responsibilities and were ready to attack. They would kill as many as possible quietly. But when the enemy was alerted, they would fight until no one was left alive, either they or their foes. To Brivel and his warriors it was not a point of concern. They knew they would be receiving greater glory after their death than when they were successful being grave makers.

They swiftly spread out as a silent human plague, sprinkling death to all they encountered. The dark air was intermittently recording the gasps of breath leaving earth, along with muffled struggles. Suddenly an alarm rang out in the darkness and the clamor swiftly escalated. Now the war would be fully engaged. Brivel felt confident the evening byzevs would be witness to their decisive victory.

However, shortly after imagining triumph, ominous sounds of a howling horde added to the plateau's cacophony. It was not emanating from human throats, but fierce sounding animals. A large pack was rapidly charging, piercing the blackness, heading directly toward Brivel's strewn forces. For the first time in his life, Brivel felt fear tightly grip his entire being. Having dispensed fear in large doses, he was not prepared to receive it. It had an immediate debilitating effect on his body and mind. He literally had very little time left either to think or act.

He briefly reflected that his formerly reliable informant was either ignorant or had deliberately withheld this lethal piece of information. Feeling as if he was moving in slow motion, he was unable to respond with calm and assurance. A sense of dread

quickly engulfed the balance of his attackers as an icy suffocating blanket. It would be over well before daybreak. Darkness was the denfengs favorite time to kill. The unsighted were unusually easy prey to dispatch.

Brivel's informer had in fact full knowledge of the denfengs, an intensely loyal breed of carnivores. The Mizar had raised and trained hundreds from birth to kill on command any whose scent they did not recognize. They had been used as guards of the prisoners for may years. Every so often, when necessary, they would have a small pack dispense with an enemy who became defiant. This would take place in sight of the prisoners present so there would be no misinterpretation of the cost exacted for disobedience.

The misinformation came from a spy named Gayluval, planted by the Mizar years ago through a planned capture. Gayluval was a perfectly motivated source of half truths. Her parents had been massacred by several Cyveh when she was a child and she wanted an opportunity to dispense justice of those who robbed her of her family.

She had dripped information to the Fruwmuxjie about the structure, the various protocols, and other pertinent subjects, and simply omitted the denfengs in her summations. Because of the denfengs' expertise, it didn't matter to the Mizar when any enemy attacked because their four-legged assassins would quickly dispense of hundreds. The furry victors would then be permitted to leisurely dine on the prey.

All of the denfengs within several miles of Sorek were brought up to the secure fortress immediately upon the commencement of the storm. They were, in many ways, the least expendable of their defenses. They and their trainers were always together and ready for any incursion.

Although Gayluval would not be aware of these pre-dawn events, today justice was served full measure on her family's behalf. She would soon be able to plan her escape from the severely wounded kingdom of terror. Perhaps she would be successful in returning home, but if not, she reached her life-long goal, and for that she would be satisfied.

REEVALUATION

As the dawn of the forth morning revealed a hazy discord of both man and nature, the balance of the forces arrayed against Sorek were now forced to calculate their strategy. Unaware of what had just transpired about their heads and beyond their ears, they would first have to access what power they had remaining before resuming any possible assault.

Because the Cyveh were the forward contingent, they were certain some of them would have died in the storm. Therefore some of the dead would be discovered before they could begin their portion of the assault. The element of surprise had clearly evaporated. Now it would be a matter of if or when they would proceed.

Messengers were sent out to the various leaders to reconvene the following afternoon at their predetermined location, several miles from Sorek. Among those able to be present were Lezun of Vigpulgs, Pazquain of Lybukom, and Yexilpar and Imixam of Eztrobel.

It was apparent to the assembled that the crucial attendee was prince Pazquain. Their kingdom's weaponry was the only reasonable alternative possible, given the present circumstances.

Yexilpar, perhaps the most able leader, begins the interchange directly, without the usual decorum.

"We find ourselves in a difficult situation. The storm has undoubtedly killed some of the Cyveh. That being quite likely, the element of surprise has been completely destroyed."

"I agree completely," volunteers Lezun. "We could easily walk into various ambushes and suffer many casualties."

Imixam adds, "It's obviously too late to mount a ground offensive. By this time they have undoubtedly retreated to the top of Sorek, which cannot be taken by any number of attackers."

Yexilpar agrees. "Although we don't know how they get up there, that is probably true. It would be a foolish waste of resources, human and otherwise, to continue at this point."

"However, there is still one valid possibility left to us," the analytical Lezun interjects.

"There is the opportunity the prince Pazquain possesses. It was our initial plan to apply their weapons after the first wave of attacks. We simply have to move it up to become our primary source of victory."

Prince Pazquain slowly rotates his head to observe the responses to Lezun's suggestion.

After a brief interlude he speaks.

"It does appear that our alternatives have diminished considerably. But I have no doubt if we launch an attack from the tree line adjacent from the plateau, we will be successful. The question becomes whether or not the Mizar can prevent us from building the necessary structures."

Although the leaders present were aware that Lybukum had their mysterious lethal weapon, none

were certain how or why it worked so effectively. They also heard that it was very dangerous, but they were ignorant of why that was supposedly true.

In addition, none of those in Lybukom assigned to use this weaponry ever divulged exactly how their baffling bludgeon worked. Nor did they disclose that fire was the only certain way to halt its mortal reach. The Lybukums simply insisted on destroying the expired enemy by fire for alleged pragmatic and personal reasons.

Withholding that information ensured that the power remained with them alone and would not be misused by the ignorant. Even a small amount of mishandling would prove catastrophic well beyond their intended victims. There were plenty of unintended pyres ignited over the years to verify that truth.

Lezun adds, "If I was in the Mizar position, I would surely amass significant power to prevent any forces to gather anywhere near the fortress during this obvious period of attack."

He then adds, "I really don't believe we will be successful no matter what plan we decide on. It's simply too late and too risky."

After considerable additional discussion, it was agreed by most to try to destroy the Mizar according to the present strategy with the amendment that they would approach from the sea.

If they could slink in undiscovered, they could perhaps build scaffolding quickly and rain on them from below and accomplish the goal of extermination.

The armed forces quickly disbanded back to their respective kingdoms. They were to gather in small contingencies in one month and meet on the eastern half of Drevkrez with custom platforms that could be rapidly assembled. The catapults themselves were already designed with that capacity, so it would only be a matter of working promptly to reassemble the primary parts and begin the attack.

BETRAYAL CONFIRMATION

As Hilophil predicted, the Mizars were far too consumed with their immediate disaster to worry about any escapees. However, what neither of them realized was the scuffle they heard as they were exiting was the initial wave of ninety well-armed eligex securing the site. If they had waited to leave even moments later or paused to investigate the matter, they would have lost all chance to escape. *"Destiny is often measured in seconds."*

Of course, each of the kingdoms faced similar difficulties. All of the forces that were poised to strike Sorek had to retreat in the midst of the unrelenting gale. Several attackers from each group lost souls through accident, misfortune, and fear. It wouldn't take the Mizars long to find the remains of the multi-force intruders and realize they narrowly avoided a massive assault from the sum of the kingdoms. This would be very unsettling to the leadership, realizing that somehow all of their enemies had agreed to work together to exterminate them. This had not occurred for centuries. Plans would have to be formulated and strategies adjusted to account for this significant change of tactics from their foes.

However, both Jovar and Hilophil knew as they were slowly winding their way to their families that they too were going to have to drastically alter their lives to survive. It was now untenable to remain in Buovonta. Neither would have the ligith branch, and they were still under the decree. The only possible remedy was to retrieve their loved ones and find a way to venture out on the Wild Sea, far from all the madness and threats that surrounded them. Neither one owned boat, but there were some fishing boats scattered along the coasts of the sea that could be "acquired" either by currency or by stealth. If the latter, they would leave some gold behind as compensation. In fact, it would be more advantageous to be anonymous voyagers to eliminate any trail that they would create through a face-to-face transaction. But *"feet are required before buying shoes."* That phase of their plan will occur at some point after the reunion takes place.

On the fifth day, Jovar begins to recognize a distinct physical feature he observed on the way into Sorek. There was a group of very tall trees piercing the sky that were clearly visible below them while they were traversing down a very high hill. As they descended into this particular valley, he clearly recognizes that distinctive grove from the opposite vantage point. He knew the temple was now only two days away from their position by horseback. They would get to investigate the temple if everything continued to go well. He immediately informed Hilophil of this new development and assured him he would be stunned by what he saw. Although revisiting the site wouldn't change any of their present situations, it would plant a very robust seed of hope within both of them. Seeds are designed to sprout if in a stable environment, even after the passing of great segments of time. *"Success germinates best within the heart."*

Over the next week and a half, the men remained very vigilant and had avoided being seen by three different groups from Sorek, which had been in transit, both to and from Buovonta. On each occasion, Jovar and Hilophel had been quietly observing all in the entourages from their vine-lined hideouts, wondering if any of the captured would be someone they had known, as remote as that proposition was.

During the second encounter, both of them quickly disappear from sight as they heard the group approaching. Jovar is emotionally staggered as he observes a former fellow consor walking casually along with the commander of the squad. They are escorting several prisoners within their column, but clearly Consor Cosmilver was not one of them. This unfortunately confirmed the long-standing rumor that there were plants within Buovonta who were actually working with and for the Mizar. He had been assigned next to Cosmilver on several occasions. They were casual friends who knew each other's families.

Without warning, a sudden epiphany struck Jovar as a thunderous shock wave coursed through his body. Cosmilver was stationed next to him on the very night that changed his life forever. No wonder he had lost men inside the wall. It was no doubt his handiwork. Jovar's instincts for retribution instantly came to the forefront. He would kill him immediately if he could—all his family too. Traitors need to die along with their families for payment of all the lives they ended and ruined.

How many other deaths was the consor directly or indirectly responsible for? How many families had to bury one of his victims? It would naturally be assumed that he was simply captured or missing in action. Apparently, he had made arrangement to move his wife and four children out of retribution's way before he wielded his traitorous knife one last time. Words were not adequate to describe the level of hate and disgust raging in the sea of Jovar's emotions at that moment. Once they passed safely by, Jovar informed his father-in-law of the wickedness he had just observed. Perhaps Jovar wasn't quite as docile as he had assumed he was becoming. *"Betrayal consumes the betrayed."*

ZWENVESTIN INQUIRY

After the women surveyed the destruction of their domain and calculated and prioritized the repair sequence they would follow, Zalin decided to go into Zwenvestin to check up on her friends to see how they fared through the adversity. Much of the town suffered damage, although no building had been destroyed. Various loose objects, such as benches in front of the businesses and homes, had been strewn about, and several had been flung to great distances.

As Zalin rounded a corner where the women often met to converse, she saw Evonquel standing by the meeting point, looking somewhat distressed, but not desperate.

"Hello, Evonquel. Are you and your family all right?"

Without hesitation, Evonquel utters a nonenthusiastic "yes," followed by a report. "All of us are uninjured, for which we are very thankful, but many of our homes are damaged by the wind and water. We will be able to repair most of it, but it will take time. I came to see if my friends would be at our common meeting place, which is why I assume you are here."

"That's right. That is why I'm here. Do you have any word on anyone else?" queries Zalin.

"Actually I'm the only one who lives in town, so we'll both have to wait until we hear something at some point. I do hope no one was injured." Evonquel's speech echoed her heart.

They conversed for several more minutes, each recounting their experiences through the deluge, adding details about each person in their respective families and giving a more detailed damage assessment. When they had completed the immediate inventory of current events, they concluded with a contingency plan of meeting again in three days. By then they should have heard about their common friends and hopefully will hear similar stories without any human casualties.

Zalin returned home to focus on the tasks before them. Early the following morning, they began in earnest to reassemble the fractured and missing pieces of their temporal existence. They began with care with the animals, repairing sections of their homes and distributing the proper amounts of grain and water.

It then became necessary to scour the various plant domains and try to salvage any damaged produce before they spoiled. They used various techniques, including preserving some in a salt solution and cooking others to the point where they could be consumed within a week. The underground cellar was also an option for longer storage because the temperature remained cool and constant once five feet underground. Surprisingly a robust amount of grains managed to defeat this adversary, and they would continue to mature until the harvest commenced.

On the third day, she ventured back to the meeting square at the appointed time to receive a report from Evonquel, if one was forthcoming. When Zalin saw her already in the square, she knew it was not all good news.

"One of Javsor's daughters suffered a broken leg when part of the barn they in were in collapsed. She will be fine in time, but it was quite traumatic. Also, Buarzel's husband was hit in the head with flying debris rounding up his horses, but he too should be all right. One of the horses ran away, and they haven't been able to find it yet. Other than that, they have the same type of damage as the rest of us. It's so good that no one lost their life in this."

Zalin was very glad to hear that no one was killed or too seriously injured. Broken bones can heal, and buildings can be repaired, but lost lives cannot be replaced. The women kept the visit brief, for each had more than enough to do for the immediate future. Exchanging hugs and bright smiles, the two returned to their homes to continue the restoration.

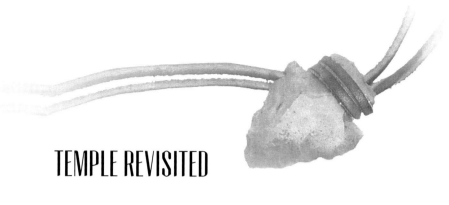

TEMPLE REVISITED

On the fourth morning from the tree landmark, Jovar recognized the place where he was taken captive. "It was right here. I'm sure of it." His mind instantly wanders back to his beloved Dohar, whom he has not seen since reaching Sorek, nor does he believe he will ever see her again. "Dohar was such a great friend. I do miss her as well. I hope they had enough sense to take good care of such a wonderful companion."

"Well, the Mizars are good at recognizing quality. They've taken enough of it from the rest of us over the centuries," Hilophil retorts.

"I need just a few moments to mentally retrace our steps. I know we have to head slightly southeast for about fifteen minutes or so, and we should come right into the temple area." Jovar almost feels like running, but he must set roughly the leisurely pace he and Dohar had traveled a couple long years ago. Because Jovar had such a keen memory, especially when he concentrated on something, he soon began to visualize the road once traveled. Hilophil follows along, keeping a sentry's eyes and ears attentive to any sign of movement other than their own. Within twenty minutes, Jovar sees the outline of the well. "We're here," he intones to Hilophil. During their previous days in the labyrinth, they had managed to scavenge enough food and water to continue, but now they will be able to eat a more wholesome fare and take enough along to sustain them easily for another week.

When Jovar reaches the well, he finds an unexpected surprise lying right where he had left it. Uncharacteristically, he had forgotten that he had left the water-carrying leather bags at the side of the well when he needed to water Dohar. He didn't take it with him for their "short exploration and relaxation tour." This find was fortuitous because in the lining of the bags was another portion of the gold he had stored for emergencies. Now they would be able to purchase two horses and a change or two of clothes from a nondiscerning character, just as he did as he began this journey. This gave him an instantaneous buoy to his spirits, but he had learned from recent experiences to keep all his senses on full alert, despite the apparent good fortune.

Hilophil's enthusiasm now became demonstrable when Jovar showed him their great gift. It was going to be very long walk back to Buovonta, but now it appeared that problem was going to be resolved. A few minutes later, they both come into the presence of the imposing structure. Hilophil stops abruptly when he sees it, obviously trying to absorb this sight in the same manner that Jovar did before him. As they begin to walk toward the temple again, they look up at the same stone in Umsnil that changed Jovar's life forever: "Out of one, many. Out of many, one." Hilophil's eyes stare at the inscription for an extended period, reliving

Jovar's experience almost exactly. Finally, he utters, "I can't believe this. How can this be? It is so beyond anything we have ever known or been told. I wonder if our histories have known this and kept it from us."

Jovar responds, "Well, I have wondered the same thing myself. There is no question that this temple shouts at us a different story than we've ever been told. If our leaders were ignorant of this, that is one thing. But if they knew of this and have not told us, that is inexcusable. In one sense, it doesn't matter because we are going to be leaving this country forever. We can start over with a better understanding of what was true in our past and hopefully revive it."

Because they were now approaching evening, they decided to go and gather some fruit from the occinal trees and venture into the interior in the morning before heading again toward their interim destination: home.

⌘

The light was scarcely perforating the dark veil of predawn, yet both men were already awake and ready to begin the hasty history course. They would have to wait for at least twenty more minutes before it would be possible to adequately view the silent sentinels still standing resolutely, declaring their allegiances to one another and their collective future. Surely if the other kingdoms were aware of this testament to tolerance and peace, they would reconsider taking up arms against those who once were their intellectual and moral kin.

As they stepped respectfully into this realm of honor and virtue, the air itself seemed to transform itself as

more pure, more gentle, and somehow more refreshing than what they had just inhaled on the external grounds. Because Jovar had already made a partial trek before a number of them, he allowed Hilophil to take the lead. Silence pervaded the initial foray into this mysterious sphere. The august nature of each figure seemed to breathe its truths into their spirits as they gazed on them. Neither had ever experienced such awe over inanimate objects before. If stones could speak, they would have listened intently. Yet even though mute, their expressions spoke to their spirits as they gazed on these carved images; most of which looked directly into their eyes.

An hour passed quickly with practically no words exchanged. Mostly sighs were uttered, either of admiration or despair. They seemed compelled to view each one with a deliberate and knowledge-seeking passion. When they had finally completed the elliptical orbit, they paused briefly at the entrance and took one last visual drink of the monuments to honor and sanity. They knew they would not come this way again. The time had come leave this sanctuary dedicated to the best of humanity and continue the advance to their futures.

As Zalin would have expected, Jovar remembered the route he had traversed in his initiation to the labyrinth. He also knew that there would be gold-loving individuals with no memories of certain transactions. On the eleventh day from the temple, they once again came into contact with sporadic humanity. Jovar had come within a quarter mile of where he entered the labyrinth. He was disappointed that he was so far off course. Experience also taught him that this section of roadways had several individuals ready to barter with no questions asked.

Within two hours, they came across a remote settlement that had several horses in a pasture. Jovar and Hilophil casually walked up to the proprietor and began to broker a deal, trading some of their assets for some of his. Although they paid two coins more than what was reasonable, and the quality of the horses were questionable, a deal was confirmed, complete with saddles, a change of clothing, and enough food to last into the last leg of their trip.

Now they would be seen but ignored as if unseen. They instantly became anonymous. There is no reason to question their movements or their normal demeanor. Obviously not wealthy, they would easily pass as local residents of no importance, which was exactly their intent. Within another two weeks, they would be standing in the presence of those they loved the most. The thought of this meeting actually occurring brought both wonder and fear in equal portions. What if something happened that would thwart this long-anticipated day? After briefly sharing their misgivings, they determined from that moment on that there would be no place for doubt to enter the room of anticipation. They will be together again soon, they will start a new life, and they will succeed and die at peace at an old age somewhere yet to be determined. It sounded like a simple-enough plan, and they would bring it to pass. Of that, they were determined.

REUNION

The intervening days of threading their way through the pockets of humanity on the various roads and villages scattered as seed on a large canvas transpired without incident. The only time small beads of sweat formed on either brow when they were approaching the entrance gates to the village where both had bid a wordless farewell. As they began to cross back through those very gates, it occurred to Jovar that he never knew the name of the village. Not wanting to venture into unfamiliar territory and engage in a discussion that would invite more questions than answers, they had decided not to stop for any food or other supplies and just wait until they arrived home.

Although their supplies were running somewhat low, the taste of soon gorging on sweet love helped suppress their physical appetites. The urge to gallop to their destination had to be resisted so as not to draw attention to themselves. Remaining nameless and faceless was still their primary objective as they rode down into the valley of dreams. That was the name Hilophil had dubbed their property when he first saw it more than forty years earlier. It was about to be fulfilling its name again.

The morning of the sixth day dawned with clear skies. The solbon illuminated a pair of travelers on the road several hours before light. Anticipation could no longer be reined in; the excitement of what was to emerge in just a few more hours was palpable. It seemed even their recently purchased transportation sensed that there was something ahead that was going to be good. Jovar felt that Dohar always knew what kind of mindset he was in. Jovar deduced that it was probably some kind of scent or body language that he was unaware of that caused Dohar to respond in the same manner as him. He began to realize that when he was fearful, Dohar would be anxious. If he was calm, so was Dohar. Reminiscing about her revisited the internal grief he carried because of his permanent separation from her.

It was early afternoon that they entered near Zwenvestin. Although they knew many people in the village, they crossed the bridge farthest away from town. They did not want to be recognized by anyone except their own family. They climbed the hill with a measured gait, still not alerting anyone that there might be an emergency. When finally crossing over the crest, the valley of dreams shone as a radiant-green emerald in their spirits.

They both saw three women working in the field nearest the house. It was close to harvesttime, and they were obviously inspecting the progress of their crops and pulling out any intruders that had managed to escape their earlier inspections. The men didn't want to be seen before they walked in on them. They

were almost near their destination when the smallest happened to turn around and glance their way. She immediately motioned to the other two to turn. For a moment, there was no motion or apparent recognition of the two strangers. But suddenly Zalin erupted into a dead run, shouting and crying simultaneously. Her Jovar had miraculously returned!

The smallest woman then began to sprint. Nesigil, necessarily running a more measured and mature pace, came in third. Once at the entrance to the house, both Jovar and Hilophil began running as well, abandoning their transporters. It appeared to the participants that time had suddenly slowed down, and they were only aware of their eyes and hearts being fully engaged. They embraced one another with such passion, joy, and laughter that they would later comment that the whole town must have heard the collision of lonely hearts being instantly transformed by overflowing affection. The initial conversation was punctuated with such enthusiastic and disjointed interaction that they agreed the back of the house would be the place to continue the details of the impossible saga.

The pace of the interchange of information resembled a verbal torrent. The stream only began to abate after about forty-five minutes. Now feeling somewhat emotionally drained, they decided to change the venue again and retreat to the house. The atmosphere inside resembled a wedding day celebration. Each respective family member was practically adhered to the other. *"Unexpected joy rejoices."*

Another hour elapsed before practical considerations entered the room. The woman practically pranced and danced into the kitchen to prepare food. This would be a feast, no matter what was served.

SEA APPROACH

A month later the boats, manpower, and materials were assembling for the stealth attack on Sorek. Meeting at the prearranged shore of Drevkrez, the dedicated crews were optimistic. Although the strike force was relatively quite small, they were precisely and succinctly equipped for the task awaiting them.

Several were well armed, but the construction workers out-manned them nine to one. This mission was to be carried out without violent interaction if possible. The purpose was to hit them from below and retreat just as quickly after their weapons were deployed, literally on the heads of the Mizar.

By the forth evening they were quietly pulling ashore under an overcast night sky. The convoy traversed quietly through the massive pillars of living wood, stopping within a mile of the edge of the forest. They would quietly wait until the next evening and set up their weapons close enough to reach the top of the plateau. Before daylight the battle would commence.

Early the next night, under cover of darkness they moved into position and began the assembly process. They had designed the scaffolds to be assembled with only ropes, and had cut various notches for each succeeding piece to fit snuggly into place. Each junction point, where the various pieces met, were covered with cloth to dampen sound.

Only those in charge of assembly were permitted to speak, and then with a hushed voice. None of the usual back and forth was allowed. They had one chance at surprise left, and this was it. They were quite vulnerable to attack and would all be killed if discovered. A large force would have been impossible to remain undetected.

All was proceeding well until a distant noise began to be heard by several of the workers. At first it was not discernable as to source or type of sound. But shortly it became apparent that a group of howling animals was rapidly coming in their direction. It was not certain whether this constituted a threat or just happened to be a random event in the middle of the night.

As the noise intensified, it did appear that the animals were in fact coming closer and didn't seem to be veering away from them. All work was momentarily stopped so they could all listen. Another minute elapsed and it was clear they would be overrun if these animals didn't alter their course.

They, too, were about to have additional insight concerning the Mizar's storehouse of living weaponry. Although they didn't realize it at that moment, they would never see daylight again. The anticipated attack soon arrived, and within a few minutes of screams, growls, and battles, the scene became silent, except for the occasional guttural exchanges between the victors.

However, the toxic batches were also present. The vanquishers soon began to devour the newly discovered menu and consumed it along with the standard fare.

Within minutes several of them began to have an epiphany of their own and quickly vomited and convulsed into eternity.

When the trainers eventually arrived later that morning, they were ignorant of the great importance of how their decisions would affect their entire kingdom. Their normal policy was to bury their faithful warriors in a place of honor on the plateau.

They were shocked to see seventeen of their animals lying dead. Several denfengs had been killed by weapons, but most had no external signs of trauma. It was quite perplexing; they had never encountered such loss of life on a routine assignment.

Ignoring what should have given them pause as to the cause of such catastrophic loss, they simply followed standard procedure. Three of the deceased were leaders of the pack. It was decided to bring them back for a burial at the established place of honor. They left the remainder of the carnage in place and headed back home. They would come back and recover the rest the following day.

Two weeks later, several sengens were gliding high above the surrounding terrain. As they approached the fortress and peered down, they didn't perceive any movement of man nor beast. They began their descent in preparation to gorge on the abundant, lifeless forms. Before long, they would be adding themselves as unwitting additions to the massive funeral site they were about to dine on.

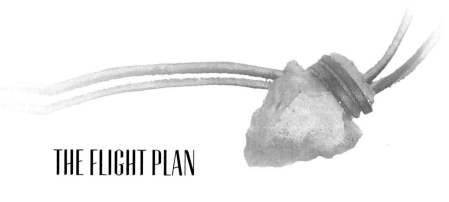

THE FLIGHT PLAN

On the third day, the conversation began to focus on their collective future. Jovar initiates the topic by reminding the women of their status. "I would like us to think about something. In case you have forgotten, Hilophil and I are still fugitives and could be arrested or sentenced to death if the authorities knew we were here."

Zalin appeared to have been abruptly struck by some invisible force. Her body involuntarily shuddered. "Jovar, you don't think they would arrest you from escaping from Sorek, do you?"

"What proof do I have that I was ever at Sorek? I don't have a ligith branch, and for as much as they knew, I simply stayed just out of sight the whole time. No, I would surely be arrested and probably thrown into the whirlpool for cowardice."

Nesigil asks her husband what he thinks of the situation.

"There is no question we can't remain here. Even if one person knew we were back, we would certainly be turned in for the reward. We must begin to plan to move far away from all of the kingdoms. Jovar and I have already made tentative plans to purchase a boat on the northern coast and leave on the Wild Sea. We have

no idea what we will find, but we know there are twenty other tribes that used to live in this area, so we might come across one of them in time."

Nesigil is shocked. "What do you mean there are twenty other tribes around? Where did you get that idea from?" The men had agreed not to bring up the discovery of the temple until several days after being home, in order to assure the women they were fully lucid.

Jovar continues the narrative, "Within two weeks of leaving Buovonta, I was traveling just inside the rim of the labyrinth and discovered an ancient, abandoned temple. There were twenty-nine inscriptions on the archway leading into the temple, and one of the languages inscribed was Umsnil. It said, 'Out of one, many. Out of many, one.' This obviously meant there were twenty other tribes that once were present that are no longer here. Perhaps they moved away for a similar reason as we have."

Zalin interjects, "We are going to have to leave everything behind?"

Jovar quickly responds, "We will take as much food as possible, at least enough to sustain us for seven months. We will, of course, take necessary tools and other items. But we will also have to give Salib to one of our neighbors the day we leave. It will be impossible to take her on a boat with us. We will put her in a pasture and leave a note. We can't leave any clues behind as to our destination. We need to wait several weeks for the harvest to be completed, and then we will depart."

Nesigil, filled with obvious desperation, asks, "What about Filoquaid? If we don't wait to hear from him, we will never see him again." Hilophil had anticipated that gruesome scenario.

"Nesigil, I promise you I will return after we are settled and try to find him. I will contact people I know who would be familiar with his whereabouts. But we simply cannot wait here. Probably the Mizars already know we have likely escaped. It will only be a matter of time before they will search where our families are located and send the eligex to find us. Actually, I'm surprised they haven't been here by now. There must have been a fair amount of escapees, and we are obviously not on the top of their list."

Nesigil responds with a flood of tears, which was atypical of her. As a matter of fact, Zalin couldn't ever recall any such demonstration of grief emanating from her mostly stoic and practical approach to all problems, great and small. However, even though Nesigil knows the truth of her husband's comments, *"a mother's heart is never far from her children."*

The balance of the conversation includes several alternative suggestions from the women, but they already knew the sad truth. Although the subject was quite depressing, the alternative was not tenable. To receive back the incalculable gift of their mates and father was too precious to risk for convenience's sake. They surely had been tempered in fires no less intense than those in the forges. Those produced weapons to kill. Their blaze produced a great zeal for life itself and would not be sacrificed for any reason within their control.

The following several weeks of preparation proceeded swiftly. Determining which items were

indispensable for survival headed the list. A variety of tools were collected. Several sturdy bags were filled with a variety of seeds that had been collected over the years to help regenerate crops. Clothing was also trimmed to several apiece. Living in a mild climate helped with the choices, although footwear was of utmost importance. Thankfully water would not be an issue because the Wild Sea housed fresh water. Within twenty-two days, the cache was completed. They would use their wagon to transport the materials to their interim destination. Once on the boat, there would be no revisiting their past, save for a promised fatherly return by Hilophel.

Although the unknown is always intimidating, the had already survived what should have been unachievable. It was also encouraging to know that the temple provided clues that there were probably tribes somewhere that had likely left for identical reasons. Although not ignorant of the necessity to defend yourself, your loved ones, and your neighbors when necessary, the temple was a clear sign that this was not inevitable. There were seasons of peace and harmony. That is how they wanted to finish their lives.

Naturally Ilistra, being a young girl, had thought of the possibility of not being able to live a normal life with others her age, and later of being a mother. Zalin had several discussions with her about this subject and assured her the temple figurines meant that there were people that they would meet and that she will eventually have the family life that they had up to this point. Although not convinced that would transpire, she did receive her father back from the dead, so was it so hard to believe that there are others living somewhere else that they would meet and become friends with? After all, she unexpectedly met Felora, Cesingria, and Juwimil, and since then has made twelve more friends.

She wondered to her mother if they would be willing to go with them. Zalin responded that it would be possible that they would, but they would be taking the unnecessary chance of possibly having her father and grandfather captured and put to death if they said anything. Ilistra knew that was the only alternative before she asked her mother, but it was a very difficult thing to imagine, forever leaving her dear friends behind. She would have to be very careful not to disclose in any way their plans of departure. And she was aware the very lives of those she loved most could be lost if she accidentally disclosed that information. *"Truth's goal is saving life, not destroying it."*

Keeping secrets intact tend to be difficult for many, but Zalin and Ilistra said nothing verbally that hinted at the coming scenario. However, when one receives such a dramatic treasure, it will manifest in spirit if not in voice. The next scheduled meeting with women quickly evolved into a series of questions directed at Zalin. They all perceived that something happened to enliven her soul. Zalin knew she has to prepare answers.

She wove a tale of receiving good news about Jovar. He would be returning within six months, both plausible and understandable if not factual. It also expediently consumed the time frame well beyond their secret departure. Although she was internally remorseful deceiving her best friends, she was planning on leaving

a cryptic note that wouldn't disclose their strategy but would communicate her love and admiration for them. However, she would have to discuss that part of her plan with Jovar. As she was more than aware, *"some farewells are best unrecorded."*

The harvest was well above average, despite the sporadic losses throughout the fields. The rainfall was adequate and timely, but the abundant crop was somewhat ironic as well. They would only be reaping enough to carry them for seven months although it was obvious the yield would easily double that. However, with a plentiful seed supply, they would be able to plant seasonal crops within three months if they found a suitable plot. The various kingdoms were mostly blessed with very good soil.

Because no one knew anything beyond the fringes of the Wild Sea, it was certainly a high-risk enterprise, but *"at times there are no good choices."* Yet Jovar was well versed in the unexpected revelation, so for him as least, it was worth jumping blindly off the cliff to see what was residing at the bottom. Hilophil was one such unanticipated, significant find. He was confident there would be more such discoveries awaiting for them.

As the final stowing of the wagon was completed and every detail carefully scrutinized multiple times, the decision was made to leave in the middle of the following night to avoid all contact with anyone. Salib was to be left free to roam the barn area where there was plenty of feed, which was also open to the pasture that also had abundant food.

Zalin knew that her friends would worry when she didn't show up for their regular visits and would surely come up to see if there was anything wrong. Jovar agreed to allow Zalin to write her note to her precious circle, but only to let them know they wouldn't be returning because of a change in orders for Jovar; the details of which were secret. But she wrote that Jovar knew she had to write them but that they were not to divulge any information about their departure because it would jeopardize all of Zalin's family. She invited whoever wished to take Salib as their own and to harvest what remained in the fields. She reminded them the authorities would eventually claim the property as their own, but they were free to take whatever they needed because they couldn't take any more possessions with them. Zalin left the note in the center of the kitchen table where they met at her mother's house from time to time.

It was about three hours before daylight when the caravan departed for a new world and existence. It would take three weeks or so to reach some of the villages scattered on the seashore on the edge of Eztrobel's western border. Because they were from Buovonta, they would not be considered hostile, nor would they likely be noticed because there was limited commerce exchanged between the two kingdoms.

Altogether, the families still have eighteen gold coins left for their resources. It was estimated an adequate boat would take about half of that amount. Jovar and Hilophil were paid one coin every three months, and Hilophil had been a consor for fourteen years, and they had been very frugal with his wages.

The boat would have to be of adequate size and seaworthy. The sail would have to be in good repair with no major defects and with several nets. If asked about their purchase, it would be said that they wanted to become fishermen. It was something both had wanted to do for a long time. Some of their ancestors were fisherman, and they felt it was part of their destiny. There would surely be a boat owner that will realize that he could make a large profit out of ignorant novices and will sell to them willingly. Once they purchase their escape vehicle, they will load their supplies at night and set sail before dawn to head downwind. The prevailing winds came from the west, so they would see their first dawn of freedom in the east on their newly acquired boat. It was appropriate that the end of their old life and the beginning of their new would commence on uncharted waters.

BEZNEZELANG

The night sky was sparkling and clear as they began their voyage. The byzevs hung as innumerable gracious necklaces suspended against an impenetrable backdrop. As each one took their prearranged place in the procession, they looked back one last time at the place they loved. All wished it wouldn't be obligatory, but they knew *"necessity is rarely convenient."*

The caravan proceeded quite slowly at first. They had both animals hitched to the wagon, making it easier for each to share the load. And although all had a place to sit in or on the wagon, each person felt the agony of the permanent separation clinging to their hearts and minds. Each chose independently to silently disengage slowly, even though it magnified their collective grief. Memories would have to suffice from that point on.

After several hours of steady progress, the light began to illumine the roadway. It was quite obvious the storm had wrecked havoc in practically every location they passed by. It was beneficial in a selfish way to see many such groups approaching them, mimicking their model. Many were proceeding to where they had left, had probably lost everything, and were returning to their families, with residual possessions on hand, to start over. They too were going to have a build a new home within the constraints of the old one many were returning to.

Every so often they would see kesereks going to or from their ordered locations or assignments, but they never stopped them to ask questions. There were far too many refugees to question. They would only intervene if it was necessary. Every time they stopped at a *xylon*, if there were others there, they kept to themselves. If they were greeted, they would return the greeting without enthusiasm to discourage additional discourse. If they were the only occupants, they would simply choose the xylon that was farthest away to communicate another tacit message to any who would happen to stop.

After dissecting many villages, they finally drove into Beznezelang, a thriving fishing village perched at the edge of the sea that creates its own unpredictable weather patterns. There were common areas outside the village proper where visitors could temporarily stay. They found a remote place to stop, and because it was approaching evening, they decided to wait until morning to go ship shopping.

Both men were already on the way to the shore at dawn. The women were more than capable of defending themselves. Although not aggressive under normal circumstances, they knew how to secure their ground if necessary. Besides being able to wield several smaller weapons, they had been taught to use a sword since childhood. They would be no easy mark.

Besides, the men were only going to be gone for about four hours in their initial foray to access the possible purchases and return to their families. The townspeople seemed to be friendly enough. Since most have the same profession, it lent itself to being well acquainted with one another, as well as a security against outside mischief. Therefore each stranger was easily and quickly identified as a possible suspect among the locals. Most were not concerned about them being dangerous, but opportunistic. Fishermen were considered hardworking, but also too trusting. The village had developed an implicit understanding: unless one had family in the town, many eyes would remain fastened on the newcomers until proven innocent. "Strangers invite scrutiny."

The men both felt that it would be best to introduce their false intensions quickly to possibly limit a lengthy, probing inquisition. To keep it businesslike would help define the parameters of the discussions and assist to facilitate a timely purchase. They walked along the sea's edge and only stopped if they saw a boat that seemed adequate.

Two hours into the hunt, they came across an apparently sound dry-docked vessel, at first glance a quite suitable form of transport for the self-imposed expatriates. It appeared all of the criteria was present from the memorized list of indispensable items. A young lad was doing some minor maintenance on the craft. Hilophil approached the youthful mariner about the object of his care. Being obtuse was not Hilophil's forte.

"Excuse me. This boat seems to be in good working order. It doesn't seem as it's been used recently. I was wondering about any possibility of purchasing it."

Pefghal was not only the diplomatic language of the loosely cooperating tribes but was also basically a second language for most of the masses because commerce was common among them.

The young boy was rather tall for twelve years old, was physically fit, and quite handsome. At first, he just stared blankly, almost sadly, at Hilophil. "Actually this boat belonged to my uncle who died suddenly several months ago. He had no family. My parents were accidentally killed several years ago, and I was my uncle's only kin. He took me in to live with him ever since my parents died. Everyone in the village knew that he desired that I would receive this boat and his other property if he passed away."

Hilophil genuinely felt sadness for him, having recently undergone his own version of loss. "I'm very sorry to hear that…?"

"My name is Minsyl," responded the owner. "Actually I have been considering selling it because although I know how to sail, I am not a fisherman. The rest who are in Beznezelang have no need of this boat, having their own vessels. Uncle Yekelon knew that I am learning to be a carpenter and not a sailor, but he still wanted me to have it as a valuable possession of his. He said I could sell it if I wanted to. He wouldn't mind."

"Well, as I mentioned, I am interested in this boat if it's something we could afford." Jovar was the silent partner in this meeting. Hilophil liked getting the point quickly and wanted to test the financial waters to see if there was any room to barter and perhaps save some reserves for their future.

Minsyl continued, "I would have to ask some of the other owners what they feel would be a reasonable price. Could you come back tomorrow and I'll give you an answer?"

"Yes, we would be happy to do so. I hope we can work something out for both our sakes." With that, the men retreated to share the news of this swift and potentially providential development.

For all of the dreadful and awful events that had transpired over the past several years, it was appearing as though good things were beginning to make their presence known at a regular pace recently. Almost fearful of believing in such a rush of good news, it was welcome nonetheless. Many of the losses were permanent, but the family was striving so the good would be just as unending.

As the deal makers communicated the essence of the potential transaction to their families, the mood brightened considerably. Although the amount may exceed their ability to acquire their escape vehicle, it did sound promising. Ilistra was listening intently as well, and knowing there were other young people around was comforting to her as well, even if it would be only a brief interlude. If they were here now, they could be there then.

The group made arrangements for food and sleep and positioned themselves under the wagon in case inclement weather struck overnight. Morning seemed to be lagging to the men who were anxious to hear from the budding entrepreneur. Apparently, Minsyl was also restless, for he was already at the site. After a brief greeting, Hilophil asked the all-important question.

"What did your friends tell you about the price, Minsyl?"

"They said it should be a hundred and twenty *spefuns* or ten gold *kellions*."

They did not have the currency of Eztrobel, but they did have the kellions, which was the common currency for inter-kingdom trading. Hilophil asks Minsyl if he could privately speak with Jovar for a few minutes to discuss the matter. They retreat about twenty yards to confer with each other.

Jovar begins the discussion. "I know it's more than we wanted to spend, but then we will have our means to escape. I don't think we should counteroffer. I'm sure all of the locals now know these outsiders are looking to buy a boat. They wouldn't like it if they felt we took advantage of this young boy. I say let's close the deal on the condition that he takes us out on it and gives us instruction on how to sail it effectively."

Hilophil, usually a very shrewd negotiator, doesn't immediately respond but thinks through Jovar's suggestion. "You know, I think you're right for all the reasons you mentioned. Let's close the deal." They had the money with them in order to wave the cash in front of him to encourage the closing of the sale. After informing Minsyl of their contingency, he agreed to take them sailing for several hours to familiarize themselves with their new seaworthy home. They mutually agree to get their lessons at the same time tomorrow morning. Minsyl will make sure the boat is on the shore ready to sail in the morning.

The next morning was a delightful day to be on the water. A steady west wind was blowing hard enough to easily set the sail and gather some speed. Initially, the two novices took turns asking the neophyte captain everything that came to their mind. They wouldn't have a tutor for long. *"Better to ask than to wonder."* After about an hour, each took turns at the rudder while the other helped direct the sail to its most efficient angle when necessary. With only a few mistakes, they soon felt somewhat comfortable with their new purchase. Of course, it was a perfect day to be out. Perhaps an additional thirty-mile-an-hour winds with pelting rain might dampen their spirits and challenge their infant expertise.

When they were all safely back on shore, Jovar asked Minsyl how far east any of the other fishermen had traveled. He replied, "Several of them have gone for over a week easterly and mentioned that the fishing was good. They said they saw the south shore at all times, but there was still open water directly ahead. Because the horizon is only a few miles on the sea, they wouldn't know how far they were from an eastern shore. Besides, the only exploration they were interested in were the best places to catch fish. They had no interest in other matters."

The men inform Minsyl that they will be loading their boat the next morning and leaving the area. Minsyl asks them the logical question. "Where are you going?"

At first, Hilophil hesitates. He then actually reveals a partial truth. "Well, we are interested in settling

somewhere that is not involved in warfare. It seems that each of the kingdoms is either in conflict or between conflicts. We simply would like to live without that ever-present threat." Jovar was taken aback by such forthrightness. Admitting the primary truth that they were escaping persecution would have likely caused the inquisitors to stop them from leaving until further investigation. "Lying is temporary self preservation."

Now it was Minsyl's turn to pause. After a brief interlude, he replies to this revelation, "You know, that sounds like a really good idea. We all go through training here regularly. It will only be a matter of time before I will be required to participate actively in either defending Eztrobel or attacking our enemies. I don't like that myself, even though it is probably necessary. It would certainly be nice to live where that wouldn't be needed. Would you consider allowing me to go with you? I have no family left since Yekelon died. I have friends, of course, but the thought of not having to constantly prepare for warfare would be wonderful."

The men were not prepared for that request. They looked at each other as Minsyl was expecting an answer. Hilophil counters with, "We would have to think about it and discuss this with the rest of our family. We will let you know by later this afternoon." They agreed to meet again in four hours.

Back at their temporary refuge, they explain what had happened. The comments were both positive and negative about the implications of taking on an unknown commodity. However, it didn't take long to realize he would be far more skilled as they with the boat.

This would be very important when difficult weather arrived. It would also be helpful to have a sturdy helper to clear land and construct living quarters. Both of the men felt he was an honest, hardworking, and pleasant boy. They all agreed that the rest of the family would have to meet him personally to make a final decision.

As expected, Minsyl was already present at the boat when they arrived. After explaining the gist of the conversation, he agreed to accompany them to meet the rest of the family. As the women saw Minsyl approach, their first impression was positive. He certainly filled all the outward requirements. Ilistra was also excited that she would have someone more her age to talk and work with. Pleasantries were exchanged, and all parties asked and answered questions to each other's satisfaction. After an hour and a half, it was agreed that Minsyl would come along. They only required him to inform his acquaintances of his decision and that is was of his own free will. They had no interest in adding kidnapping to their resume.

FROM SHORE TO SHORE

The expeditionary force began loading the boat well before dawn. There was a real enthusiasm for this day. *"Yesterday is not an option, therefore today beckons."* Within two hours, all of the gear was safely stowed. They ate their last meal on the beach and unceremoniously shoved off in search of their future. A light westerly wind was blowing, which was sufficient to make slow progress. As the day wore on, the winds would become stronger, and progress would be multiplied.

They were about thirty minutes into the voyage when they saw their first solbon rise from below the horizon. The pale-orange sphere soon caught the clouds on fire, and all aboard the craft felt it was a good sign. They understood that this happens every cloudy morning, but this was not just any morning; it was their morning. They also had prepared to shelter themselves from an unrelenting sun or persistent rain. Several tarps were erected near the back of the vessel to protect them from overexposure from either phenomenon. The coverings were also adequate for inclement weather, having been treated with wax.

The south shore revealed the dotted settlements from time to time. They also observed the dramatic rise of the cliffs. They knew they would eventually see the fortress of the Tyvrens high upon their perch as they continued their eastward crossing. When they neared evening of the first day, Minsyl steered closer to shore so they could anchor. They had decided that they would sleep on land from time to time as conditions permitted. They were not in a race; they were in quest of their destiny. There was also the adventurous side of seeing formerly unseen land and realizing they would undoubtedly see much more than they imagined as time progressed

On the fifth day, the fortress began to appear in the distance. Because of the severity of the cliffs, it was impossible to scale them, so there was no need to have forces stationed below. There was an adequate force within the bastion to repel any intruders that might try to attack from the sea. Although there had never been any recorded attacks from the water, they did have sentries overseeing the liquid field, in case any such attack would be forthcoming. There were fishing boats regularly passing by and were easily identifiable. When the group passed by two hours later, there was no cause for alarm for either parties.

Day eight began with a chill. Brisk winds from the north with plenty of dark, menacing clouds pushed the front along. They had not yet stepped ashore, but Minsyl immediately began to sail for the shoreline. North winds almost always meant at a minimum rough waves and oftentimes followed by severe storms. Because they were always well in sight of the south shore, they beached within fifty minutes. It was none too soon.

They disembarked on a sandy portion of the beach and secured the anchor onshore to keep the vessel from washing out to sea if the storm became severe. They saw a squall line approaching and secured several tarps to protect their supplies. Two tarps were quickly erected in some nearby trees to provide protection from the coming rain. Thankfully the winds remained reasonable and the rain plentiful, but within two hours, the system passed them by, and the weather improved dramatically. It was becoming abundantly clear that taking Minsyl along was a very wise decision.

Once they crossed over the eastern edge of Eztrobel, they entered an unknown realm. None of the kingdom maps extended beyond their border. This phase was true exploration. As several days passed, the terrain on the south shore gradually descended from the high cliffs to rolling hills and then to flat plains.

On the third day of observing these grasslands, they determined to have lunch on the shore and perhaps explore a little. They knew they wanted to establish their new life in a place where there was suitable soil for planting that also provided some cover from the sea and the weather. They wanted to be hidden from anyone sailing by them. They also required a location that would help them survive a massive meteorological onslaught that provided some extra protection from what they had recently experienced. This terrain didn't qualify, but it would be nice to take several hours of being on land and relaxing for a while.

There was a gradual incline from the sandy beach area to the grassy plain. When they disembarked, they realized that the grass was actually higher than themselves. This precluded any casual exploration. One could easily get lost in no time, which was not on anyone's list for the day. Nevertheless, there were a few scattered trees within walking distance, which would provide shade. It was agreed to rest under a rather large tree with an expansive crown about a hundred yards from the water's edge that had patches of grass surrounding it.

Once under the tree, they immediately noticed a well-worn path leading from the tree into the high grass. It was quite clear that this area was inhabited, either by animals, people, or both. The revelation cast an unsettling atmosphere for lunch. Although the thought of following the trail had crossed their minds, it was far too risky to take a chance of what they might find. They ate rather quickly and departed the site within twenty minutes.

Once navigating around the grassy fences circling the tree, they were stunned to see six well-armed men in a semicircle around their boat silently staring at them. It wasn't clear what their intentions were. It also wasn't apparent as to their origins. They were adequately dressed but not in any attire they were familiar with. To compound the situation, it was evident to the boat guards that the vessel owners were unarmed. It crossed Jovar's mind that to be killed in this manner would be worse than remaining a prisoner to the Mizars.

While still fifty yards away, Hilophil instructed the women to stop and wait while the men closed on the uninvited intruders. However, the plan dissolved instantaneously because emerging from the just-departed tree were six other well-armed men closing from behind. Hilophil instructs the women to rejoin them quickly.

The options were quickly disintegrating. Hilophil whispers to Jovar, "If they mean to do us harm, we'll have to offer them our goods. They may let us live and leave if we willingly give them our possessions. We'll stop about ten yards from them. Let me do the talking."

After halting at the predetermined distance, Hilophil offers a nonthreatening explanation with the itinerary in Pefghal, hoping for the best. "We are traveling to a distant shore far from here. We stopped to eat and rest, and we were going to continue our journey when we saw you."

The lead man, still staring, responds to Hilophil's statements, thankfully understanding the language. "What tribe are you from?" Hilophil reflects for a moment that this would be a good time to be able to read someone's mind. There's probably only one good answer, and the chances of him giving it are not excellent. "Well, sir, we're really not from any tribe. We have been persecuted and are trying to start a new life without hurting anyone."

The inquisitor looks rather satisfied with the answer. Perhaps they have more in common than a language. "Do you have any proof of what you say?"

Hilophil responds, "The boat you're surrounding is all of our worldly possessions. Doesn't that speak to our intentions?"

The man folds his arms and puts his right hand to support his chin, apparently weighing the answer. "Yes, I suppose it does."

Hilophil then asks the all-important question, "Do you intend to do us harm?"

"No, we don't. We were taking precautions that you weren't intending to do us harm."

A wave of relief literally washes over the assumed victims as a refreshing, gentle surf. Hilophil then requests, "Are we free to go?"

"Yes. But would you mind if we visit with you for a few minutes. You are the first people we've seen for some time that has stopped in our realm."

Hilophil accepts for the group. "Yes, we will stay for an hour if that's acceptable to you."

The leader nods his approval.

⌀⟩⟩⟩⟩⟩⟩

The group they stumbled upon numbers several hundred. They established a large compound several miles into the grasslands but keep a small rotating contingency near the shoreline as an early-warning system. They too are peace loving and have escape plans in place to disappear in the foothills that lie beyond their present location. Their origins were from the far southeast several generations ago, when a small group fled fighting among three other tribes they were associated with. Their tribe was the Umgesu.

After an hour and a half elapsed, Hilophil thanked the Umgesu guests for their hospitality and kindness and, with friendly faces, pushed off to continue their journey.

Once back off shore, the men speculated that the tree was probably a lookout for ships passing by. Minsyl advised they go farther out from shore than normal to have an adequate distance between themselves and any possible hostile forces that might try to overtake them. All agreed, and within an hour, they were about a mile off shore. This would make any person onshore unable to see them clearly and would made it practically impossible to follow them either. Later in the day, they decided not to go ashore again unless they were seriously considering a possible site to put down foundational roots.

THE THIRTY-NINTH DAY

Midmorning of the thirty-ninth day, they suddenly saw something they hadn't observed as of yet. Still well in the distance, barely peeking about the horizon, land was appearing. Still traveling about a mile from shore, they knew they must been seeing a coastline. Because it was only a few miles to the horizon, they knew before much time has passed, they would be setting foot on an eastern shore.

By early afternoon, they were now within a quarter mile from the shore. Looking to their left, the shoreline extended beyond their sight. They assumed it would probably go on for many miles. They turned their launch parallel to the shore to observe the terrain and the general flow and contents of the surrounding land within their view. The earth hosted plenty of mature trees that would be essential for building. It was a gentle, rolling landscape that also had larger patches of cleared ground, which would make planting much easier if the ground is fertile.

They explored for another several miles when they came upon a gently flowing river emptying its contents into the sea. They all agreed to land near this site for closer examination. They set foot on the property at about dinnertime. They ate quickly so they would have

time to travel upstream along the southern bank of the river to see what lay beyond their eyes.

They stayed close together, chatting as they went, observing this and commenting on that. There were no obvious signs of human habitation, which was comforting. They had no intention of becoming isolationists, but they wanted to meet by design, not happenstance. After thirty minutes, the land flattened and opened up. Before them lay a fairly large lake, the source of the river. To say it was beautiful would not describe the scene. They walked up to this reservoir and knelt on its sandy shore. Several edible birds that had been floating nearby quickly flew skyward. A sign of lunches to come?

Standing on this pristine shore made them begin to feel all the effort they had expended was well worth it. There was no question they would be staying to do more investigation, and their hearts were beginning to whisper, "Welcome to your new home." The apprentice crew had smiled from time to time at clever wit, but the faces usually dispatched the grins quickly, granting them a very brief existence. Presently, each one had a broad, sustained grin that spoke contentment. They proceeded back to their vessel to prepare for a second, more leisurely meal and then search for a nest on the ground to curl in. The anchor was secured to the shore with an additional rope tied around a convenient tree for added safety.

PLANTING NEW ROOTS

The after-breakfast discussion centered around going some distance up the shoreline to see what else might be ahead of them, which might be more appealing. The majority favored starting to settle upriver as soon as possible. Time was not really their ally after all. Food was adequate for several more months, but no one could live under a tarp for any extended period. Jovar, the constant explorer, was the lone mild dissenter. After a few more minutes, they convinced him that it would be better to build where it was more than adequate to meet their needs than spend more energy searching for essentially the same thing. Once established, they could explore for weeks up the coast if they wanted to. They could even rebuild if it surpassed the present choice by a large margin. Even if they did decide to relocate, they would have a permanent base to travel to and from during inclement times. The agreement was then unanimous. The work would begin in earnest the very next day if the soil was productive.

The next morning, they dug up soil around the lakeshore and to the tree line. It was very dark and moist and had the earthy smell to it that they were accustomed to. The work would proceed. In the interest of secrecy, the first order of business was to hide the boat from any potential seeking eyes. But before that could happen, all of their supplies had to be carried to the field by the lake. This took most of the day.

There was still several hours of daylight left. They observed a series of high-growing, dense shrubs that were close to the shore about a quarter mile south of them. After inspecting the site, they decided they would fashion some skids from some smaller trees and attach one of the pulleys they had taken along to a larger tree to pull it into position. Within six hours on the second day, they accomplished their goal. The boat was close to them, out of sight, and available within several hours if they needed it. The boat had a cover designed for it, so it was secured to keep the elements at bay.

⟨⟨⟨⟩⟩⟩

The sixth month had passed since their landing. Two structures were weather worthy: one for the human cargo and the other for their supplies. The outbuilding was also divided so that the produce could be kept there as well. They had planted within days of their arrival, and some of the produce was not far from harvest. Although much had been accomplished, more was left to do. The mood was one of almost-constant joy. They had succeeded against tremendous odds and had found a place that was spectacular, both for the body and the soul.

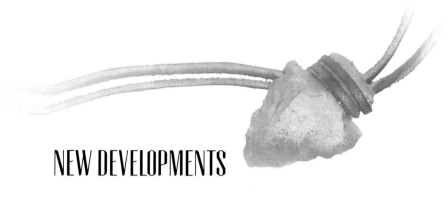

NEW DEVELOPMENTS

By the third year, they were a viable colony. Once it was clear they would survive, Hilophil reminded Nesigil of his promise to her. He would ask Minsyl to escort him back to where they had departed so he could try to find their son. Nesigil sorely missed Filoquaid but knew that the chances of ever finding him were next to nothing, and she couldn't bear to lose her husband a second time. She had to trust that they had raised their son to be honorable and trustworthy and that he would be a wonderful father. Her main regret would be that he would not know that his father had survived and the family was reunited.

She released him from the promise. Reluctantly Hilophil agreed not to pursue the issue further, although he was fairly certain he would eventually be able to find him. He thought perhaps in a few more years, Nesigil would give him permission for his sake so he would know he tried everything possible to bring his son home.

During the fifth year, Jovar came into unexpected contact with another group of mariners that resembled them not that long ago. Jovar spotted them several miles up the coast while hunting for local game. He was by the sea and would glance occasionally from the

shore and look in both directions. While just within the tree line, he spotted them. He watched them for over two hours before drawing any conclusions. They seemed identical to themselves in need and intent, so he decided to make contact on the beach they were temporarily harboring on.

He approached from where he had spotted them so they would quickly see him walking on the shore. He had left his arrows and bow behind where he could find them. He didn't want to come close to them armed so as not to needlessly alarm them or force them to decide if he was friend or foe and act accordingly.

When he came within thirty feet, he stopped, lifted his right arm by his head, and revealed his palm to them. This was a universal sign of friendship. He spoke in Pefghal, the only other language he knew besides his native Umsnil. "My name is Jovar. I live here with others. I mean you no harm. Is there any way I can help you?"

Although several of the men staring at him were armed themselves, they made no attempt to threaten him. There were several women and children present as well. They were not from any tribe that he could recognize. However, the man closest to him replied in Pefghal.

"My name is Koprah. We also mean you no harm. We have traveled from a great distance to try to find a place to settle down. We came from the far west to settle away from the violence that surrounded us."

"How far west did you come from?" inquired Jovar.

"We've been traveling east for seventy days."

This meant they were some distance west of the kingdom of Drevkrez. Jovar has another question. "How is it that you speak Pefghal?"

"My parents taught us. They said they had learned it when they were children. My parents fled to the west and settled in an uninhabited area, only to find the conflict eventually follow them. We decide to move far enough away so we could escape the turmoil for good."

This new development was both promising and potentially risky. As he was well aware, not everyone can get along. He thought of a possible compromise. Jovar decides to dispense some cordial advice. "I come from a colony not too far from here. It would be nice to have friendly neighbors around. May I suggest you keep traveling up the coastline for a couple weeks or so and look for a place to settle down? Just like us, you need space to grow. You are the first people we've seen in over five years, so it's quite likely we are the only ones in the vicinity. You want peace, and so do we, so it would be good if we respected each other, gave each other room to grow, and eventually visit from time to time."

The supposed leader responded that it might be something they would consider. When Jovar was speaking, he sensed that the balance of the party was receiving his words. He bid them farewell and good fortune and mentioned that if they did take his advice, he would look them up someday so they could begin a pleasant relationship. Without further delay, Jovar excused himself and began walking up the coast. This too was a chapter written that would affect them at some point, hopefully in positive ways.

The next several years were developmental for both settlements. The group did take Jovar's advice and built a similar compound with a similar layout. They had visited each other's property and lent each other a hand when they were able. They also shared their seed with each other to diversify their crops.

However, those weren't the only hands that were extended. Minsyl and Ilistra both grew physically and emotionally. They had weathered the same intense challenging period as friends. Now they were at the point that it was becoming more than friendship. Rather than try to hide their emotions, they approached Jovar and Zalin about becoming husband and wife. Of course, Ilistra's parents weren't blind and could see the relationship come into flower over the years. Minsyl proved to be a perfect gentleman as well as a skilled artisan. They gave their blessings. It was the custom of the time for the father to give the man his daughter's right hand if he first promised to be faithful for his lifetime to her and had a history of being a responsible man. The ceremony took place on the beach where they all had stepped into their futures.

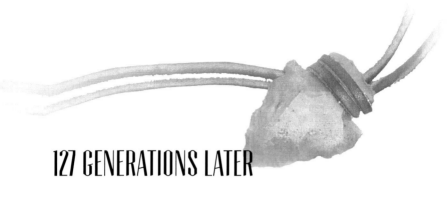

127 GENERATIONS LATER

Starili could not restrain her enthusiasm for exploration. Majoring in archeology, she loved uncovering the past to get clues to ancient cultures' lifestyles, dwellings, and beliefs. The current expedition had been periodically working a larger geographical area for many years, and recently they had been dissecting subsections in promising locales. The section Starili was assigned to was in its initial plotting phase. Local tradition spoke of a lost civilization's buildings that had been identified by earlier cultures as being in this particular area, but no one was able to find them. The area was prone to earthquakes, which meant that the buildings were quite likely destroyed and completely grown over.

It was Starili's responsibility to lead a team to a quadrant to be surveyed for initial mapping, which was about three and a half miles from the main camp. She was to travel due north, and her team was to fan out within sight of each other and look carefully for any signs of any structures that may be protruding from the ground.

Four hours into the search, Starili commanded everyone to break for lunch. There were only three main choices for seating: on the ground, on the vegetation,

or on a rock. Starili looked to her right and noticed what looked to be a possible edge of a rock protruding from some very thick vegetation. Although it was covered with a heavy coat of brilliant blue-green moss interposed with random vines, it had the appearance of being one of thousands of rocks entombed by the vegetation in this overgrown jumble of greenery. As she sat down, it was quite firm, another indication that she had found a nice, secure place to dine upon.

After chewing on some high-protein, dried meat, coupled with several dried apricots, with plenty of specialized fluids to avoid dehydration, she casually reached for a stick and removed some of the moss entombing the apparent stone she was sitting on. Suddenly she observes a perfectly straight right-angled edge that had to have been man-made. Yelping with excitement, probably having made her first real discovery, she called for the team to assemble around her.

Now faced with a legitimate artifact, she threw her stick down and instructed the team to take their specialized tools from their backpacks to slowly and carefully work to remove the moss and vines. After a brief examination into the dense greenery beyond the makeshift chair she had been sitting on, it was apparent they had stumbled upon a mostly horizontal, completely engulfed, elongated structure. Dr. Squaver, her professor, had thoroughly trained each staff member. Therefore he told the team that if they uncovered something, they were free to carefully proceed until he was present. He knew from experience the thrill of those moments and encouraged the novices to participate in firsthand-revealed history.

Starili wanted everyone present until they could discern some further proof of man's fingerprint on this piece of stone. She too understood that everyone in the group is part of this discovery. Once the initial removal is under way farther down the structure, she was in position to slowly help remove the veil over the front of the rock. After several minutes of careful dissection, she discerned some sort of script beginning to emerge from the face.

She excitedly reassembled the force together for all to see. The teams yells and pumps their arms in a victorious celebration. She then asked for two volunteers to go back to the main camp to retrieve Dr. Squaver. Lilly and Melossia, her two best friends, gladly volunteer for the mission.

Four hours later, the doctor arrives, happy for this moment. By this time the face has been wholly disclosed, and a satellite station is set up to send the now-digital inscription to the main office to see if there is any information as to the writing's origins. Now that there is hard evidence that some sort of structure is in the immediate vicinity, Dr. Squaver orders the main camp be moved to this location for a complete and thorough dig.

Within four days, the home office has sent a reply back to the anticipatory group. The language is know an Umsnil. The inscription reads, "Out of one, many. Out of many, one." As the group ponders this cryptic

message, Starili has no idea that with a casual flick of a stick, what she has inadvertently discovered is herself.

The following fall Starili is enjoying a paid leave of absence for her first pregnancy. Her husband Jackson is appreciative for the extra time they have to spend together and has been preparing the meals because Starili is close to her due date. The conversations regularly revolve around the soon-to-be addition to their young family.

"Well, I hope this baby is going to be like you," volunteers Jackson.

"Why do you say that, Jack?" responds Starili.

"It's just that you have such a zeal for life and never take 'no' for an answer. Hopefully our daughter will have the same kind of enthusiasm and talent you possess."

"You know as well as I do, we want her to be her own person, and will be happy for whatever gifts and personality she has. By the way, I still am working on names for her. Last night I rearranged the letters in my name and have come up with this. I want to know what you think about it."

She slowly hands the paper to her husband while looking directly into his eyes, her face expressing a slight pursing of her lips. He smiles and glances down at the writing, contemplating the name he has just been introduced to.

"Ilistra...I haven't heard that name before, but I think I like it. It sounds creative and adventurous to me. What could be better for our new daughter than having the same letters in her name as her mother? I think we should go with your idea."

Two and a half weeks later, early on January ninth, snow falls outside a frost laced window, gently swirling in a celebratory dance, welcoming a new baby to her first dawn.

The father, cradling little Ilistra with the first of many embraces, smiles as only a new father can and whispers to his mate, "By the sound of that strong voice, she may just have what it takes to follow her mother's lead."

With a tired grin, Starili responds. "We'll see Jack, we'll see."

EPILOGUE

Every nation, like-minded group, and individual have two things in common: a final authority and a list of good and bad, right and wrong, true and false. These beliefs and principles are usually encoded in official documents, statements, and creeds—or simply inscribed within the soul.

Because these convictions and codes differ from nation to individuals, the consequence will ultimately and necessarily involve conflict. The most common form of disagreement manifests in the form of debates and discussions. However, occasionally, the dissimilarities are so passionate and antithetical that the shedding of each other's blood is the outcome.

Individually, we are in the process of composing our own chronicles. We largely determine how our autobiography reads, but none of us knows when our story will end or can anticipate the inconceivable. The events that impact us beyond our ability to control alter the narrative, and a sudden epiphany can revise our journal entirely as it did for several of the characters.

The choices we make usually have an effect beyond the borders of our territories. The sum of those decisions will only be fully known when our personal face stones are unearthed to be read and deciphered, both in this world and the next.

The book of Revelation
Chapters 19-22

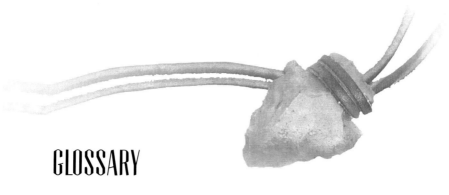

GLOSSARY

ackbisk. Military commanders who were immediately under Prince Madnak

agjolin. A very hard and extremely rot-resistant, dense wood

alisorn. A very hardy sweet berry encased in a thin shell

Balequo. Overseer of the qualungs

belixium. A very hard, straight wood found in extremely high terrain

bexalars. Warriors of the kingdom of Qyisilinks

biosal. Repository for the diverse flora and fauna of Buovonta

Brivel. Prince of the kingdom of Fruwmukjie

brvistin. A very dense, iridescent, black stone

brugon. Highest military commander under the prince of Eztrobel

Buovonta. One of the kingdoms that bordered Sorek to the south

byzevs. Evening stars

Calsweold. Imaginary land

colstone. A light-blue, dense stone often used for walkways

cons ponder. Dense hardwood tree

Cyveh. A lethal, lightning-fast snake, also a moniker of the Fruwmunjie warriors

dengfengs. Midsize animals that were aggressive defenders of their owners

Drastrilon. A name for the prince of Mizar

Drevkrez. Northwestern kingdom

eligex. Sorek's elite soldiers

emelicon. a sour sauce that congeals when baked

ezmeniad. An iridescent light-green, granite-type stone

Eztrobel. One of the kingdoms of the loose confederation

Fajixa. The Mizar language

Fangore. One who oversees the transfer of prisoners from their original posts

fasingbuk. A four-legged, gentle creature about three feet high at the shoulder

feklors. Small, agile creatures that like to climb trees and move quickly

felcon. One responsible for securing the prisoners once they arrive

Filoquaid. Zalin's brother

fogol. An animal raised for meat

forgal. Administrator in the kingdom of Buovonta

Fruwmunjie. Kingdom of the Cyvehs

furens. Sorek war machines, which hurl fiery capsules at enemy positions

Galdering. Imaginary heroine

Gevruges. The fortress of the Lybukom

goniclis. The various prisoner-holding facilities

Heoprel. Village where Jovar is exiled from

High Council. Mizar leaders who assign all citizens to their duties

Hilophil. Zalin's father

Ilistra. Daughter of Jovar and Zalin

Imixam. Prince of Tyvrens

inbengs. A select few sodii, chosen by the consors, who help direct combat

Jelwark. Name of the felcon responsible for securing the prisoners

Jovar. Son of Rawlgoul and Xenvel, husband of Zalin

juxul. An animal similar to a ram

Kanka. A furry little animal similar to a rabbit

kesereks. Common Tyvrens foot soldiers

Kilrek. Fortress which Prince Madnak oversees

Klimpend. Village designated for military strategy sessions.

Konquid. One of the twenty-five provinces within Buovonta

krespind. Fruwmunjie gates that have embedded razor sharp-shards on its exterior

krunun. A very large animal, although fierce looking, and is actually a herbivore

labyrinth. The extremely dangerous territory between Sorek and some other kingdoms

Lashsborg. Village that housed a facility for the infirm and insane

levik. Midlevel officers of Eztrobel

Lezun. Leader of the Vigpulgs

ligith. Branch from a tree that only grows in the kingdom of Sorek

Linrox. Province where Vaumond was born

Lybukom. Potent westernmost kingdom

Madnak. Prince of Kilrek

magi quills. Round-looking creatures with long, blue-green hair

Mizar. Founding tribe of the Fortress Sorek

Meyungulas. Kingdom of exclusively female rulers

morvengs. Highly infectious vermin

motvear. Common sodus who serves under the fangore

Nesigil. Zalin's mother

Nocvals. Common Mizar soldiers

occinal. A sweet fruit than is often dried for its longevity qualities

okwillian. A large bird of prey, known for its great speed and stealth

opirsak. A ramming device to puncture stone walls used by Sorek

Pazquain. Prince of the Lybukom kingdom

Pefghal. Diplomatic language of the eight loosely affiliated kingdoms

prelivins. Soft, loose-skinned rodents similar to puppies

privos. Leader of the Mizar High Council

prosalutar. Highly esteemed military veteran from Buovonta

philmons. Assigned by the High Council to oversee forty Mizar families

qualung. One who has failed in his assignments

qinsab. A recorder secretary for the military and keeper of their archives

Qyisilinks. Far southwestern kingdom

sanifligs. Skilled craftsman

Selbon. The village within the province of Konquid

sengens. Very large, carnivorous bird

solbon. The sun

Sodus. A common soldier

sodii. Two or more soldiers

spignock. Striking stones used to create sparks to start a fire

splik. A measurement roughly equivalent to a yard in length

spinitic. A prolific type of softwood tree, common in Buovonta

squalingas. A wingless bird with bright yellow feathers

swomtig. Watchmen on the walls of Eztrobel.

syncryse. Amalgam that creates the swords of Sorek

Tyvrens. Tribe from the kingdom of Eztrobel

Umsnil. Language of Buovonta

valins. Well-trained sodii awaiting promotion to consor

Vaumond. Head of the High Council of Mizar

vesmor. A very dense rock with varying light to dark red appearance

Vigpulgs. Northwestern most of the eight kingdoms

vijinct. Chief overseers of the warriors of the Vigpulgs

vosmelic. A poisonous material absorbed by the skin that results in swift death

vsirun. Wooden shafts of the arrows

Wisgraf. Overseer of all education in Buovonta

xorol. Bright-blue stone laced with black streaks

Yel Corum. Weapons forge center in Buovonta

Yexilpar. Prince of Eztrobel

Yihami. Native language of Meyungulas

zagin. A courier of Buovonta

Zalin. Jovar's wife, daughter of Hilophil and Nesigil

Zilquani. Language of the kingdom of Lybukom

zilvah. A type of grain used primarily in baking breads

zinying. A tangy berry

Zwenvestin. Village where Zalin was born and raised